LOVE KILLS

D1553425

LISA RENEE JONES

ISBN-13: 978- 1091111462

BE THE FIRST TO KNOW!

THE BEST WAY TO BE INFORMED OF ALL UPCOMING BOOKS, SALES, GIVEAWAYS, TELEVISIONS NEWS (THERE'S SOME COMING SOON!), AND TO GET A FREE EBOOK, BE SURE YOU'RE SIGNED UP FOR MY NEWSLETTER LIST!

SIGN-UP HERE:
HTTP://LISARENEEJONES.COM/NEWSLETTER-SIGN-UP/

ANOTHER SUREFIRE WAY TO BE IN THE KNOW IS TO FOLLOW ME ON BOOKBUB:

FOLLOW ME HERE:
HTTP://BOOKBUB.COM/AUTHORS/LISA-RENEE-JONES

DEAR READERS

Love Kills picks up right where *Love Me Dead* left off. Lilah Love, our resident bad-mouthed FBI profiler is in a faceoff with the Umbrella Man. A serial killer who is wreaking havoc in New York, killing women, and getting Lilah's attention in all the wrong ways. There are parts of this case that just can't be ignored are pointedly for Lilah herself. This is no ordinary serial killer, but when has Lilah ever attracted an ordinary serial killer?

This case first opens up with Lilah's current boss, Director Murphy, calling Lilah to inform her that her former mentor Roger Griffin asked for her assistance on three murders. But when Lilah turns up at the current case, she soon learns Roger never called for her, he's not even involved in the case, which is singular, not triplicate, but this case is too gruesome, and her happenstance upon it, is too peculiar to let go. So, soon, Lilah has taken jurisdiction, over not just the one victim, but another who died in her arms. Both poisoned. Both with pristine homes, which was unlike them. Both holding umbrellas forced in their hands. And now, loved ones of theirs are dead too. The local detective on the case, Lori Williams, who doesn't match the victim appearances at all, soon goes missing, causing another wrinkle in this case, which worsens when her boyfriend kills himself in court. A mark of the serial killer, which is to force the loved ones to kill themselves.

While Lilah is navigating her first case back in New York City, she's also navigating her relationship with the infamous Kane Mendez. They toe a fine line between her badge, and his family's cartel involvement. They're the worst match on paper, but in the real world they're made for each other. And while this case is reminding Lilah why she does what she does for a living, Kane is reminding her how good they are by welcoming her back into the home they once shared—her clothes right where she left them. But Lilah and

Kane aren't the roses and unicorn type of couple. No, amidst this insane case she's working, and his missing uncle who runs the cartel, Kane has assigned one of his men to closely watch over Lilah much to her absolute refusal, but Jay isn't going anywhere, despite her best efforts to threaten him away. Though shockingly, as the case progresses, he proves himself helpful and loyal time and time again.

Eventually, Kane and Lilah end up at a high-society event in "support" of her father (as much support as she could ever give that man), to make a statement, that they're back and a force to be reckoned with. But soon, this even leads right back to Lilah's case with a dead pig making an appearance which relates back to the massive amounts of pig's blood found at the first crime scene. Just as the case is heating up, Kane has to leave, and Lilah is left trying to figure out which way is up and which was is down with this case. Does it relate to her? Is this just some sick and twisted individual? But the scene at her father's event, the victims' likeness to her old friend, Beth Smith, who was also mysteriously called to the first crime scene as the medical examiner, and then subsequently shipped off to Europe because of said likeness to the victims, all of it just doesn't set right with Lilah.

So she sets off to do what she was trying to avoid, she sits down with her old mentor Roger, who has input himself into the case, to work through it how they used to. But on the tail end of that brainstorming session, when Lilah is on her way home, she knows this is the night Umbrella Man will strike again. And so he does. In an alleyway, she's at a standoff with Umbrella Man, a victim, and Detective Williams. Just as bullets begin to fly, Jay leaps in front of her to save her and gets shot, and she's now walking toward the figure she believes is the killer and all the answers right along with him...

INDEX

Lilah Love (28)—dark-brown hair, brown eyes, curvy figure. An FBI profiler working in Los Angeles, she grew up in the Hamptons. Her mother was a famous movie star who died tragically in a plane crash, which caused Lilah to leave law school prematurely and eventually pursue a career in law enforcement. Lilah's father is the mayor in East Hampton; her brother is the Hamptons' chief of police. She dated Kane Mendez against her father's wishes. She was brutally attacked one night, and Kane came to her rescue, somewhat, and what unfolded that night created a secret between the two they can never share with anyone else. This eventually causes Lilah to leave and take the job in LA, away from her family, Kane, and that secret.

Kane Mendez (32)—brown hair, dark-brown eyes, leanly muscled body. He's the CEO of Mendez Enterprises and thought to be the leader of the cartel that his father left behind when he was killed. But Kane claims his uncle runs the operations, while he runs the legitimate side of the business. Lilah's ex from before she left for LA. He found her the night of her attack and shares that secret with her.

Director Murphy (50s)—gray hair, perfectly groomed. Former military. Lilah's boss. The head of the LA branch of the FBI. Sent Lilah to the Hamptons to follow the assassin case.

Rich Moore—blond surfer-dude looks, blue eyes. Works with Lilah. He and Lilah were sleeping together until Rich wanted more and Lilah called it off.

Jeff "Tic Tac" Landers—Lilah's go-to tech guy at the FBI.

Grant Love (57)—blue eyes, graying hair. Lilah's father, the mayor, and retired police chief of East Hampton. A perfect politician. Charming. He's being groomed by Ted Pocher to run for New York governor.

Andrew Love (34)—blond hair, blue eyes. Lilah's brother and the East Hampton police chief. Andrew is protective and seems to be the perfect brother. The problem is that he's perfect at everything, including being as macho and as bossy as their father. There's more to Andrew than meets the eye.

Lucas Davenport—tall, looks like a preppy version of Tarzan. A very successful and good-looking investment banker, he has taken to hacking in his spare time. He is a cousin of sorts to Lilah and Andrew. His father was the stepbrother to Lilah's father. His father was also known to be with Lilah's mother, Laura, on the night they both disappeared in the plane crash. He flirts mercilessly with Lilah, seeing as they're not blood-related, but she always shoots him down.

Greg Harrison—Lilah's old partner from the New York Police Department. Currently in a lot of hot water with Internal Affairs over an incident that may or may not be of his own making. He was partnered with Nelson Moser prior to being put on leave by IA pending further investigation but has been working independent security with Moser in the meantime.

Nelson Moser—a lowlife police detective who offended Lilah on numerous occasions before she moved to Los Angeles. She is not very fond of him, and the rumor circulating about him is that he's a dirty cop.

Laura Love—Lilah's mother. Famous actress. Died four years ago in a horrific plane crash. She infamously portrayed Marilyn Monroe in an Oscar-winning performance. Much mystery still surrounds her death and will be a recurring issue throughout the series.

Ted Pocher—billionaire CEO of the world's fifth-largest privately held conglomerate, Pocher Industries. Has taken a liking to Lilah's father in hopes of furthering her father's political career. He tried to do business with Kane and Mendez Enterprises but was turned down because of his rep for shady business deals.

Beth Smith—blonde, tall, thin. The new medical examiner in Suffolk County. Lilah's friend from back in the day. Beth is working one of the assassin murder cases.

Lori Williams (40s)—detective in charge of the first crime scene in *Love Me Dead*. Went missing shortly after and is connected to the Umbrella Man case. When we left off, she was in the alleyway with Lilah, Jay, and the Umbrella Man.

Ralph Redman—Williams' boyfriend, criminal attorney. He killed himself while in court. A victim of Umbrella Man.

Jay—Kane's man sent to watch over Lilah. Was shot in the final scene of *Love Me Dead*.

Thomas Miller (30s)—redhead from the forensics portion of the investigation.

Sally (50s)—gruff, wild brown curls, works at the station.

Lily (25)—petite, brunette, research girl.

Chief Houston (30s)—Lilah knows him from back in the day. Is currently working with her on the Umbrella Man case. They butt heads, but they're amiable.

Kit—tall, brooding, fit Mexican man who smiles big and kills easily. Security guard for Kane's apartment.

Melanie Carmichael—new medical examiner dealing with the case while Beth is overseas.

CHAPTER ONE

It's as if time stands still.

Jay, Kane's idea of the bodyguard that I don't need, is now lying on the ground bleeding out, while I'm running down a dark alley toward his shooter, gambling that I'm not about to bleed out with him. Gambling that this person in front of me, dressed as a woman and holding an umbrella, doesn't want me dead, too. Gambling that this is, in fact, the Umbrella Man, who wants to keep playing games with me. Gambling that I'm about to be close enough to use the gun in my hand and shoot the fucker, with the intent to kill him, and do so with a smile on my face.

I'm halfway to my target, the person and that umbrella, when a hard, loud crack sounds, echoing through the alleyway, the origination source impossible to pinpoint.

"Get down, Lilah!" Jay shouts, and I consider the very real possibility that the Umbrella Man is behind me, or worse, the sick fuck has another sick fuck helping him kill people, and that sick fuck is now behind me. In which case, Jay is all but dead, and the woman in front of me, really is a woman, not the Umbrella Man, meaning she needs my help.

I launch myself toward her, and the instant I'm in motion again, another crack breaks through the stiff rain-laden air, seeming to come from right in front of me. I can feel the moment that bullet zips past me. He's fucking firing right at me, testing me, pushing me, trying to scare me.

I don't stop moving, but a part of me gives him what he wants. I react. I brace for impact when I normally wouldn't give a fuck. Clearly, that's changed, and I know why—Kane fucking Mendez. I fucking want to live for Kane. I don't want to leave this earth because of that man, and I hate him right this minute for making me a scared little bitch. I hate scared little bitches. Another crack sounds, and this time, I'm certain the sound is coming from above. Instinct has me

7

looking upward, scanning rooftops, when suddenly, the person in front of me crumbles to the ground.

Fuck.

Fuck.

Fuck.

That's not the Umbrella Man.

"Call an ambulance!" I shout at Jay and then I forget about protecting myself.

I lunge for the person sprawled on the pavement to find it *is* a woman, an umbrella over her head, along with her hands, which I assume to be taped to the handle, as was the case with the prior victim. Thunder roars above, and more rain begins to pelt down on me in cold droplets, but I push onward. I kneel next to the victim who has lipstick smudged all over her face and a bullet hole in her chest, a hole gushing blood. Nothing about this fits what I know of the Umbrella Man who kills with poison. I check for a pulse, and there isn't one.

"Take cover!" Jay shouts. "Take cover."

I ignore the warning because let's face it—if the shooter wanted me face down and bleeding out, I'd be face down and bleeding out. My focus is now on the eerily silent Detective Williams, who's still tied up in the corner, no longer shouting out warnings. I grab my flashlight, shining it toward her location to find her slumped over, which I'd bet my crime lord Latin lover, who says he's not a crime lord, means she's dead. I jerk my flashlight right, standing as I do, searching the dark shithole of an alleyway, that feels like it's about to swallow me whole.

A movement, or more a shift in the air, has me swinging back to my light left, when suddenly a man comes from above, jumping to land a foot in front of me. By the time he's steady on his feet, my weapon is steady in my hand and pointed at him, right along with my light. Un-fucking-fortunately, his gun is pointed at me as well. I'm a good shot. He's better.

I blink to confirm that the most notorious assassin on planet earth, at least that's still living, is standing in front of me. A man who recently did me and Kane a favor, which means nothing. A favor from this man won't stop him from killing you the next time.

"What the hell are you doing here, Ghost?" I demand, because this man doesn't play games about killing. He just pulls the trigger, and yet, he's wasting time pointing a gun at me.

"Saving your ass," he says, "say thank you."

"I can save myself, which includes killing you and becoming a hero."

"A hero to who?" he asks.

"Everyone you might kill in the future, which we both know will be many."

"But you won't kill me," he counters. "You're too like me to want to see me fall."

Too like him. It's not a statement that I wear easily, but it's one I wear too well for comfort. "Did you kill those women?"

"Yeah, honey, I killed them. They were both booby traps. It was you or them. Look for yourself." He shines a flashlight on Detective Williams' hand, where it dangles near the ground, a gun taped to her palm.

"Her finger is right above the trigger," he says. "The minute you tried to move her, she'd shoot you. It's really a clever setup if you get the time to study it and appreciate the thought that went into it."

And knowing all this, that bitch, a member of law enforcement who vowed to protect and serve, called me forward, lured me in.

"She didn't take her oath seriously, now did she?" he asks, reading my mind. "She lured you further into the trap."

Which makes me wonder if she was involved in this, if she felt safe. If she was playing the victim. If she was *him*. My gaze jerks back to Ghost. "And the other one?" I demand.

"She was booby-trapped, but that was irrelevant. I showed the other one mercy. He poisoned her. It wasn't going to end well for her."

"You show mercy?"

"Even I do, indeed, put a wounded animal out of its misery."

9

I move on. "How do you know he poisoned her?"

"I saw him set the whole thing up."

He saw *him*.

A statement that says Williams wasn't the Umbrella Man. "And you let this happen?" I challenge.

"I don't get involved in other people's business."

"And yet, here you are," I say dryly. I don't wait for a reply. "Who is he?"

"Sick fuck had paint on his face."

"But it was a man?"

"It?" He laughs. "Yes. It was a man."

Now he's just pissing me off. "Why the fuck didn't you shoot him?"

"I *don't* interfere in what isn't my business."

"You just shot two women."

"Once you were involved."

I don't even hesitate. I close the space between me and him and shove the muzzle of my weapon into his chest, my flashlight beaming into his face. "You just shot two women. That's involved."

"You're my business."

"I am *not* your business."

"I've decided that you are."

"I should shoot you just for saying that," I warn, and I mean it. He's a killer. Interest in me is trouble.

"And yet, we both know you won't."

"You underestimate me if you think I won't," I counter.

"I don't underestimate you, Lilah Love. I understand you."

Sirens sound in the near distance, approaching quickly. "Who hired you to kill me?" I ask, going where his interest leads me.

"No one."

"Who hired you—"

"You're asking the wrong question."

The wrong question.

What the fuck is the right question? Because I know that he's not Umbrella Man, and yet—he's here, and so is

Umbrella Man, and that can't be a coincidence. "You're setting me up."

"I just saved your life."

"All right then. How much to kill the man in the makeup?"

"That's your question?"

"No," I snap. "It's someone else's, but answer anyway. How much to kill—"

"For you, it's free. I just need a name."

"Are you serious right now? If I had a name, I'd kill him my damn self. What good are you?"

"I do always wonder why a killer hires a killer."

"And here I thought you didn't play games," I counter.

"I don't play games, Lilah Love, and you know it."

That's exactly what he's doing, playing games. It doesn't sit right in my gut. In fact, it makes me wonder if the victims could be hits he's organized to look like victims of a killer that isn't. It makes me wonder if I'm one of the targets. Nothing else explains why this man is here or the content of this conversation.

I shift the light from his face to just his eyes. "You don't want to cross—"

"Kane?" he challenges.

"*Me*, asshole," I say. "You don't want to cross me because I don't give a fuck where you land or how bloody the view. He does."

"You think Kane Mendez cares how bloody he gets? Interesting."

The sirens rip through the air, and vehicles screech behind us. Ghost backs away into the darkness. He's betting that I won't stop him. I could shoot him. I could arrest him. I decide to let him go.

For now.

But he hasn't seen the last of me.

And I haven't seen the last of him.

CHAPTER TWO

Rain splatters on my shoulders, while just behind me, the voices and footsteps of emergency crews echo in the dark night, made darker by cloud cover. I ignore it all, aware of the killer I just let back away from me, my flashlight and senses homed in on the alleyway, right along with my weapon. Movement to my right catches my attention, and I watch as Ghost scales a fire escape, far too quietly, invisible to anyone who doesn't know he's there. He's showing me how Umbrella Man got here and left.

I swipe the light away from him before someone else sees him. He came here for a reason, and his reason is my reason for letting him go. Whatever that proves to be, whoever is behind his presence here tonight at the same time as Umbrella Man, I need to know. And it won't be dealt with by way of the men and women in blue. I do one last scan of the alleyway with my flashlight and weapon just to make sure Ghost is gone, though I feel no danger. Not now. Not to me, at least. Ghost didn't want me dead, or I'd be dead. Umbrella Man didn't want me dead, or I'd be dead. Cold comfort, perhaps, but really, I'm not one of those girly girls who needs comfort at all. It's all about facts to me. Cold hard facts. If Ghost comes for me to kill me, I'll embrace the killer inside me. And I'll show him a woman isn't an animal to be put out of her misery. He'll be the one who dies.

I give that bitch of a hellhole alleyway my back to find the EMT crew now kneeling next to Jay and a rush of law enforcement. "Two dead!" I shout out, flashing my badge. "Agent in Charge. This is my crime scene. Secure the area now and draw a wide perimeter."

The officer nods and takes off running. Another three uniforms stop in front of me, none of them familiar faces. "Who's in charge?"

Not a one of them steps up, or even offers to play that roll, and I just start spouting orders. "Time is not on our side. Victim number one is one of ours. I know her data. I need to know who victim number two, center stage, is now. This guy kills his victim's families. We aren't going to find identification on her. Get me a team to fingerprint her and get me her name and address now." I point to an officer. "You. Do it now." He nods, and turns away.

I focus on the rest of the crew. "I need tents up now. I need forensics teams in here now, before the rain washes away everything worth seeing. I need lights. I need photos. I need evidence bagged. I need it now. Who's making the calls?"

"I got it," one officer says, holding up a hand and already hitting the button on his shoulder, that controls a microphone. Finally someone fucking does something other than get rained on.

"Get me the officer in charge," I say, "and get moving now!" With that, I dismiss them all to kneel next to Jay, who grabs my arm. "You're a crazy bitch," he chokes out. "They might as well not even save me. Kane's going to kill me."

Spotlights blast into the alleyway, and I note the pale line over his lip, a stark contrast to his dark skin. "He told me not to kill you," I tell him. "He's not done with you."

"*Wasn't* done with me," he says, letting go of my arm, his eyes shutting. "Wasn't," he whispers. "He is now."

I should be bothered by how afraid this man is of Kane. I'm a fucking FBI agent for God's sake, but it's not an emotional blow. It's not a shock. It's just Kane. I know the man is refined and handsome, well-spoken and polite, but he's also brutal. Because I'm brutal. *I understand you,* Ghost had said to me. He doesn't fucking understand me. And I *am* bothered by Kane scaring the fuck out of Jay. I lean in and whisper in his ear, "You took that bullet for me. No one gets to fucking kill you. I won't let them."

When I pull back and look at him, there's a twitch to his lips, his attempt at a smile that is never fully realized. I eye the EMT who answers my unspoken question by saying, "He's lost a lot of blood."

Translation: the vultures are already circling above, and the grim reaper is ready to reach through the ground and yank him to hell because that's what people who run with me and Kane do—they go to hell. Only, I plan to scratch the devil's eyes out on the way down. Jay won't do that, or he wouldn't have saved me, so I just have to do it for him.

Therefore, I pin the EMT in a stare and reject his bullshit secret answer hard and fast. "Save him," I order. "You fucking save him or someone will have to save you from me. Understand?"

His eyes go wide, and he nods quickly, a response that says he's clearly aware that I mean what I'm saying. Which is smart on his part because I really want to kill someone right now. I should have killed Ghost. Why the fuck didn't I kill Ghost? I could have found the instigator in all of this with him dead in the ground. I push to my feet, determined to go hunt his ass down again. An officer rushes toward me and offers me a NYPD raincoat that is big enough that I pull it over my thinner version of the same type of coat, yanking the hood over my soaked hair.

"What's the ETA on the medical examiner?" I ask, shoving my arms into the jacket and pulling up my hood.

Before the officer can answer, I hear, "What the hell is going on?"

That demand, delivered in a snarly voice, has me turning to find Houston barreling toward me like a linebacker.

He shouldn't be here is the only thought I manage before he again demands, "What the hell is going on?"

His out-of-character stabbing question hits ten nerves, and anyone who knows me, knows I don't have ten nerves to spare. "I just called this in. Unless you're my new stalker, and—and this is a big and—also the invisible man—who last I heard is being played by Johnny Depp, if he gets his shit with his ex cleaned up, of course—you can't know about this crime scene yet. It's not possible. And yes, that's a fucking accusation. Do with it what you want, but explain yourself and now."

"I don't even know what the hell that means, Lilah," he snaps, and I swear his body is all but twitching with his effort to contain his agitation. And the thing is that Houston is a chill and Netflix kind of guy all the damn time. He doesn't get agitated. He doesn't twitch. Unless that's how he's dancing, and I don't think he's dancing at a crime scene, though I've seen a lot of weird shit when people are stressed since taking this job. "This is my city," he adds. "You get that, right?"

"And my case. My jurisdiction."

His lips tighten. "My city, Lilah. My job. My responsibility. And as to your question: I was nearby. And funny thing about having you and a serial killer around at the same time is that the mayor continues to breathe down my fucking throat. It keeps me on edge."

"How *the fuck* are you here, Houston?" I repeat.

"I have an alert set for anything Lilah Love, which I'd tell you was to be supportive and that shit aside, I'm protecting my ass, too. You make everyone, including the mayor, act like a little bitch ass whiner. What the hell is going on?"

"You know what's going on," I say, not happy with his answer. "He struck again."

"If you mean Umbrella Man," he replies, "since when does Umbrella Man shoot random men on the street?"

"He didn't randomly shoot a man on the street," I snap, though he's hit another nerve. Who the hell did shoot Jay? Because Ghost doesn't shoot to maim. He shoots to kill. "Jay was with me," I say. "And he got between me and Umbrella Man."

He steps closer. "You saw him? He showed himself to you?"

"No," I say flatly. "I was going into the alley to save the two women he had captive. Jay tried to stop me. That earned him a bullet. The bottom line right now is that he's alive, but we have not one, but two dead women."

"Two? There are two?"

"I already said that," I reply. "Yes. Two."

"Holy hell." He runs rough fingers through his light brown hair. "Holy fucking hell. And clearly, they were meant as gifts for you. This is Kane's place, right?"

"You know where Kane lives?"

"Oh, come on, Lilah. He's Kane Mendez. His father was—"

"I know who his father was, Houston. Are you surveilling him?" I hold up a hand. "Don't answer that. I don't have time to be as pissed off as you're about to make me. You're correct. Umbrella Man didn't choose this location by accident, because apparently, everyone knows where the fuck I live. The victims were booby-trapped to kill anyone who tried to help them."

"Meaning you," he supplies, but he doesn't wait for an answer. "But you outsmarted him. You're still alive. You won."

"He won, Houston, or Jay wouldn't be bleeding out while two dead women decorate the alleyway with bullet holes in their chests."

"Bullet holes? What happened to poison?"

"This was a twisted game," I say, "with many moving pieces." I leave out the part where one of those moving pieces includes Ghost. "He didn't plan on anyone but me leaving that alleyway alive."

His gaze narrows, his attention sharpening. "And yet you did. What aren't you telling me, Lilah?"

He thinks he's cornered me, but I snap back with a punch he shouldn't expect. "Detective Williams didn't make it out. She's one of the victims."

His face lifts skyward, jaw clenching, and it's a good thing we're under the overhang, or he'd have a mouth full of rain. And I'm pretty sure rain in New York City has rat shit in it, which is why you keep your mouth shut. His is not, but he remedies that when he levels me in a stare and purses his lips like a chick about to go at her man. I am not his man. "Williams is in that alleyway?" he confirms, blame in his voice.

"Don't ask that question like I did this shit. Which I would have. I'd have killed that bitch if I'd gotten the chance. She tried to kill me. She tried to lure me into a trap. She called me. She knew what was waiting for me."

"Are you telling me that she was Umbrella Man?"

17

"No," I say, because Ghost named a man in makeup, but I can't know that. Not where Houston's concerned. "My guess is he promised her she'd live if I died." I pause to consider who shot Jay all over again. It could have been her, but I can't be sure. "Or, she was his partner," I continue. "She wasn't in this alone. There were shots fired from above."

"None of this adds up to a serial killer."

"Because you know serial killers so well?" I challenge, reminding him that I'm the profiler.

"I know enough," he rebuts. "What the hell happened to poison? He kills with poison."

"We don't know how many times or ways he's killed," I say. "He kills how he kills. We just might not be in on the secret codes."

"Sir," an officer says, "the press is here."

"Of course, they are," Houston replies. "Block them the hell off. I want this area sealed so tightly that a dog in heat could be right here with us and a pack of wolves couldn't get to her. You hear me?"

"Yes, sir." The officer rushes away, and Jay's ambulance pulls onto the road.

"I need to deal with the press, and the boots on the ground before this gets out," Houston says, scrubbing his jaw. "And call the damn mayor, which is one big pile of shit I need to dive into. I'll find you when I have my head that he's about to take off reattached to my body." He doesn't wait for a reply. He turns away and starts walking, stepping into what is now a downpour all over again. I don't move. Not because I'm worried about getting wet. Water doesn't bother me. Bullshit does, and I can smell it, like the stench on my shoe last week when I stepped in dog shit. I couldn't figure out where the smell was coming from until doodoo was smeared all over the fucking floor. I cleaned that up. I need to clean this up.

Ghost clutters up my mind.

Why was Ghost here?

He didn't want me dead. He didn't want Jay dead, or Jay would be dead.

I rotate and look toward the building I now call home with Kane and realization hits me. Oh fuck. Ghost was here for a reason, and if that reason wasn't me and it wasn't the victims—oh fuck, I think again. I grab my phone and dial Kane. "Hello, beautiful," he answers. "I'll be there in five minutes."

"Listen to me now. I'll explain later, soon. Turn around. Don't come home. I'm safe. You are not. Do it now. *Now.* I need you to do it now."

"Turn right," he orders his driver and then he's back. "Done. Talk to me, baby. What's going on?" His voice is calm. He's calm. He's always so fucking calm.

"Ghost was here, and he didn't come for me. That means—"

"He came for me," Kane says, finishing my sentence.

CHAPTER THREE

He came for me.

Kane makes those words spoken about an assassin hunting him sound oh so cool, calm and elegant, the way Kane manages to make all things brutal and cold sound. The man could literally say "I'm going to kill you" in that low, accented male voice of his, and make death sound like seduction. And then he'd kill you and never think about you again. Me, I do what I already did to a man—just shove a knife in your chest over and over, let Kane bury you, and then worry that my enjoyment in killing you means that I'm fucked up.

He follows his cool observation about Ghost by asking, "Is Jay with you now?" almost matter-of-factly, as if he's debating inviting Jay to dinner with us, because, of course, why wouldn't he? It's not like he has one killer hunting him while another hunts me. Or maybe it's the same killer. Either way, dinner with Jay is off the table. Maybe forever.

Fuck.

Maybe forever.

Because he took a bullet for me instead of just letting me play the damn game I would have won.

"Lilah?" Kane presses, a slight hint of urgency in his voice, a slight tell I doubt anyone but me would hear. It pisses me off. I'm pissed off at Kane. Why the hell was Jay following me around like a puppy dog?

"If you mean my *bodyguard,* he's now in an ambulance on his way to the hospital," I say. "And he's in that ambulance because fear makes people do stupid things. He was so fucking afraid of you that he did something stupid."

"What does that mean, Lilah?"

"He tried to stop me from doing my job and saving a woman in the alley. That didn't end well for him."

"And you shot him?"

"I didn't shoot him, Kane. What kind of bitch do you think I am?"

"The kind that takes killing as seriously as she does protecting those she doesn't want to kill."

"We walked into a trap set for me," I say. "It appears that Umbrella Man didn't appreciate Jay interfering. Therefore, Jay ended up with a bullet in his chest."

"How bad?"

"Bad," I say grimly. "Really fucking bad, Kane. He thought he was saving my life, but I was never in danger. Now, he thinks you'll kill him."

I can almost hear his grimace. "Lilah—"

"I told him he was wrong about you."

"Did you?" It's not really a question but rather an accusation.

"Of course, I fucking told him you wouldn't kill him. So don't fucking kill him." And with that command, I move on. "This is a game being played with me, and Jay got caught in the middle. Which means Jay can't die. If he dies, I can't kick his damn ass for being stupid."

"He's not going to die, Lilah," he says, his voice low, rough, filled with understanding that proves, once again, he knows me better than anyone else knows me. He knows I'm worried. He knows that while I can kill, while a part of me enjoys it a bit too much, those urges have yet to drive away my humanity, the way I sometimes worry they have his. Until he worries about me, which is why Jay was following me around. In those moments, in this moment, I'm reminded that he has to have a human side to see mine. And all this human crap is pissing me off. It's dangerous. We're dangerous to each other.

As if proving my point, Kane adds, "I'm coming for you. We're circling around to the flower shop one street over. Meet me there in three minutes."

"Fuck no. Damn it, Kane. Stay away. I have a job to do here."

"Umbrella Man hit one block from our fucking apartment," he says. "And Ghost was there?"

"Yes, but—"

"No but about this, Lilah, and if you need this in your own language: fuck no, Lilah. Nothing about that says you stay there without me. I'm coming for you. Don't make me walk to your fucking crime scene and drag you out of there. Ghost is a killer of killers."

"Is there any part of you that gets that I made it years without you, Kane? Or is your ego so damn big that it's going to make your head explode one day and then I'll have to get two caskets to bury you."

"You were never without me, beautiful, and you know it."

"Right. My stalker who did a whole lot of shit to piss me off. Don't do more now. Stay away. Ghost and I stood across from each other pointing guns at each other. I told you. He didn't come here for me."

"He showed himself to you. He damn sure came for you."

"He could have killed me. Hell, I could have killed him, and holy fuck, I wish I would have, but I wanted to know who hired him. Who hired him, Kane?"

"I'll let you know after I talk to Ghost," he says, and I can hear the rain pounding his windows.

"You think he's just going to tell you?"

"I know he will," he counters. "Ghost doesn't warn his victims. He has another agenda."

"I'm not a fucking idiot, Kane. You not only said and I quote 'He came for me' but you just diverted your car for a reason."

"I'm a man of abundant caution. You know that, Lilah."

"You're fucking an FBI agent, Kane. I wouldn't call that abundant caution."

"I do more than fuck an FBI agent, beautiful. And who better to protect me?"

"Careful or I'll think *you* have an agenda," I say.

"Many where you're concerned, my love, and you know it."

"Are you trying to get me to shoot you instead of Ghost?" I don't wait for a reply. "We both know—" I stop midsentence, my gaze rocketing to a glint of steel off the rooftop catching in the artificial lighting of the emergency crews, a stab of warning in my belly.

There it is again.

Another glint.

Fuck.

He's still here, and I'm not even sure if I mean Umbrella Man, Ghost, or both. All I know is one of them needs to die today.

"Lilah?"

At Kane's prod, I force a reply. "I have to go, but do not come here, or I swear to god I'll shoot you myself, someplace painful but not deadly. In the hand. Hands bleed a lot."

He says something in Spanish that sounds really fucking dirty. The man just made that about sex. Jesus. I hang up, and I'm already shoving my phone in my pocket. I step out from under the overhang, into the pounding rain, and rather than reach for my gun, an obvious move someone like Ghost would spy, I keep my hands free and ready to act. I dart across to the pavement, bypassing the crime scene. Hurrying to the side of a fire truck, I round the building and pull my weapon. Freshly armed, I enter the alleyway that runs on the opposite side of the building that sported the rooftop flash of steel. And I'm not alone. I feel it. I feel *him*. I flatten myself against the wall and watch the rain hit the pavement, darkness swallowing the droplets until the moment they make contact. I don't move. I barely breathe.

I just watch and wait.

Seconds tick by that turn into minutes in which the cold weight of my jeans hangs heavily on my legs. The control freak in me that my father has called "ridiculous" often in my life, too fucking often, wants to force the next move. I want to own this crime scene and the person who created it, but I rein in my energy, forcing patience. Something that, oddly, most people don't seem to believe I possess. They're wrong. If I didn't possess patience, I really would be a killer.

There's a shift in the air, a charge interrupted, as thunder erupts with such sudden force that the wall vibrates behind me, while the rain seems to pour from the sky. It's the distraction whoever is in this alleyway with me uses and uses well. The asshole piece of shit I'm hunting slams to the ground on two solid feet right in front of me.

CHAPTER FOUR

Whoever is in front of me might as well be invisible.

There's a fucking black hole of darkness swallowing me alive, but instinct is one of those rare friends that I actually tolerate. It kicks in, and my weapon is instantly aimed in front of me, but at what, or who, I don't have a fucking clue. A second later, an open umbrella all but pokes my eye out. I don't even think about shooting wild and not because I'm one of those little bitches who freezes under pressure. I'm not. Evident in the way I stabbed a man a few dozen times after being raped. I'm okay with killing someone if they need to die, but I prefer to see them when I pull the trigger or shove the knife in their chest. Then I know they're the right person. I know they deserve what they get.

I shove aside the umbrella, ready to find that confirmation, but my attacker is already running away, which makes *him* the little bitch. I lift my weapon and step into position to shoot, but something deep in my belly says no, don't shoot. But I want to shoot, *I want to shoot*, but something feels wrong, really fucking wrong.

"Damn it," I murmur, lowering my weapon, launching myself after the runner, barreling through the storm, watching the umbrella-wielding fool clear the alleyway.

I'm there right behind him, a streetlight giving way to a full view of his hooded frame when he runs straight into a WWE-sized man in a NYPD rain jacket. The officer catches the runner's upper arms and holds him in place. "What are you doing, kid?" he demands.

Kid.

Thank god I didn't shoot. And thank fuck, the rain faucet is abruptly dialed back to a sprinkle.

"I just wanted to see what was happening!" the kid screams. "I just wanted to see what was happening. I'm sorry! I'm sorry!" The kid starts rambling in Spanish.

"Agent Love," I announce, stepping beside the officer, his hard features turning harder as his gaze lands on me.

"I know who you are," he bites out.

"Good," I say, reading between the lines. He's heard trash about me, and he believed it, and he apparently operates off of secondhand information, which tells me what I need to know about him, none of it good. I eye the "kid" who can't be more than a pre-teen. "Name?" I say, bypassing a lame effort at Spanish, because cursing in Kane's first language, and at Kane in his first language, is where my true skills lie.

"Diego," the kid says. "I'm Diego, and I'm sorry. I just wanted to know what was going on. I didn't want to get in trouble, so I ran."

"Where do you live, Diego?"

He recites an address a few blocks away. "My mom told me to come see what was going on."

I doubt that, but I don't care how he got to that alleyway. I care about getting him out of here. "And if we take you home right now, will your mom be there?"

"Yes," he says, "Yes. I swear. She wanted me to see what was going on. She didn't know I'd come down here to where the police cars are. She's a good mom. Please don't think she's bad. She's not bad. She didn't know I'd do this!"

In other words, he's where he shouldn't be and he's afraid of getting in trouble. I might feel bad for the kid, but I could have shot his little ass. The Umbrella Man could have shot him. I lift my weapon to show it to him. "I could have shot you," I say. "Somebody else would have."

He starts to cry. Typically, I prefer making grown men rather than kids cry, but in this case, it's good. The kid needs to cry. He needs to shit his pre-teenage pants. Me and this badge have seen shit, bad shit. Nasty shit. The premise of scared straight needs to be put to work right here, right now, while he's just a good kid who did a stupid thing.

He's also not the person I felt in that alleyway. Someone else was there.

I cut the officer a look. "Take him home and confirm his story. And make sure he doesn't have a record."

At this point, two additional officers have joined us, and the officer holding the kid hands him off to another and says, "Do as she said." He then faces me, pulling off his hood to allow me to see his sharp features, shaved head, straight nose, and the splay of lines by his eyes that ages him to at least forty.

"Sergeant Morris," he says. "I'm the ranking officer."

Ranking officer with an attitude. A common illness that I usually blow off, but I'm not blowing him off. In this moment, I decide that I don't like him, and not just a little but in a deep, instant, profound way. I also don't like that he's here, by this alleyway, when it's technically not part of the crime scene. "Clearly, ranking officer makes you above taking the kid home." I pull down my hood, as well, and eye the scratch on his face, down his cheek. "What is it that you have to say to me, Sergeant? Because you obviously have something to say or you wouldn't be squaring off with me."

"I wasn't aware that I was."

"Because you're standing here, staring me down, to do what? Ask me out for coffee later?"

"Kane Mendez wouldn't like that, right?"

"Ah, there it is. The bullshit I've been waiting on. Does it shoot just from your mouth or from your ass, too?"

"I'm the guy who keeps things real."

"Real, is it? Well then, let me join the 'keeping it real' party. If Kane Mendez is all you got, you'll have to think harder on ways to rattle me. Like perhaps eating the last donut when I'm at the precinct. Why are you back here by this alley instead of securing the scene?"

"I saw you run in this direction and thought you might need backup."

It's not unbelievable, if someone else said it. From him, it's bullshit and ten kinds of bullshit in fact. "Secure the alley," I say. "Do we know who the victim is?"

"Detective Williams."

"The *other* victim," I say.

"Not yet. We printed her."

"I need an update on those prints, now."

"Of course," he says, smirking. "And a broader search of the area?"

The smirk gets to me.

I like to smack smirks off faces. That I let him keep his, really does speak to my restraint, which is better than most believe. If I smack you, it's not emotional. You deserve it.

"Home our resources, here, on the crime scene," I say. "I don't want any more mass hysteria than we already have with the mayor's recent press conference. Keep the scene tight." On that note, there are two dead bodies waiting on me, and they are certain to be better company than this man. I turn away and start walking.

"You don't want to sweep wide for a suspect?" he calls after me and then murmurs, "Why can't the FBI just let us do our fucking jobs? One of our own is in that alleyway."

I whirl around and face him. "One of your own? Williams called me into that fucking alleyway into a booby trap. So if that's who you're calling your own, asshole, you now know why I'm in charge. So, do as I say, or get the hell out of here."

His jaw clenches. "Williams wouldn't do that."

"And yet," I say, "she did, so if you want to go wide with this search, cause hysteria and talk to the press, she'll be the villain. The police will be the villains when one of your own is killing innocent people. If you want that, we can put you on camera to deliver the news."

"I don't believe Williams would do that."

I step closer to him. "How do you know? Were you fucking her?"

"No. I was not."

"Did you *ever* fuck her?"

"No, fuck, no."

But he cuts his eyes. "How personal is this to you?"

"She was one of us."

"That again? Then I'm a lying little bitch, is that what you're saying?"

"I'm saying, Williams wouldn't do what you say she did."

"Then I *am* a lying little bitch."

"I'm saying—"

"Don't repeat yourself. I'm not stupid enough to need to hear that again while you appear to be stupid enough to keep repeating yourself. Leave. You're too involved to play an investigative role."

He cuts his stare, his jaw tightening to the point that it might snap before he eyes me. "I want to stay. I want to help."

"Who hurt you?"

He frowns. "What? I mean, we dated but—"

"But you didn't fuck," I challenge. "When was the last time that you 'didn't fuck'?"

"We *didn't* fuck."

"And you didn't avoid my question. You're cut. Who cut you?"

"A served warrant gone wrong."

It's a quick answer, too quick, and his eyes shift slightly. He's lying when he has to know I can confirm his story. Which has to mean he's stupid, and if he's stupid, he's not Umbrella Man, but Williams wasn't him either, even though she tried to lure me into the alleyway. To the game. I think of the family members of the victims who Umbrella Man has used and abused. In every case, he promised someone close to the victims that if they did certain things, they could save the person they love. But if Morris was being tormented, if he was being promised that he could save Williams, he knows she's dead now.

"Agent Love."

I look up to find an officer standing to my left, his rain hood pulled low. "There's a man at the west perimeter insisting he see you," he announces.

Kane.

It's going to be Kane, and I'm going to kill him before Ghost has the chance.

"I'll be right there," I say, and when I turn back to Morris, he's gone. I look toward the dark alley, my gut pulling me there again, but Kane is here. He couldn't just stay away. What part of Ghost is here trying to kill him does this asshole not understand? I turn away from the alley and look for the officer who announced my visitor, but he's gone.

I start walking toward the west barrier he indicated, vowing not to hurt Kane until we're alone, without witnesses.

I cut through the gaggle of law enforcement, answering questions I didn't intend to answer, finally breaking away to a clear path when my phone rings and I grab it, glance at my brother's number and hit decline. Rain begins to pelt my shoulders again, and I yank up my hood, walking toward Officer Brad Henry, who I know from the past. "Brad," I greet, stepping in front of him.

"Lilah fucking Love. I heard you were the Queen Bitch of the Night."

"And I heard you still parked a donut shop in your belly," I say, motioning to his ever-present belly and back up at him. "I see that rumor was true."

"Twins," he says, rubbing his donut shop.

I move on before I don't move on because the man is supposed to be able to run, fight, and protect innocent lives. He can't even protect himself. "Where's my visitor?"

He frowns. "Visitor?"

"I was told that I have a visitor here to see me."

"No. Not that I know of." He shouts out to another officer behind him and to the left, next to a patrol car, "Travis! Any visitor for Agent Love?"

"Nope. No-go on the visitor," Travis calls back.

No visitor.

A bad feeling hits me, and I turn away from Brad, pulling my phone from my pocket and dialing Kane. "Lilah."

"Where are you?"

"At the flower shop where I told you to meet me. Where are you?"

"You weren't here?"

"No. Should I be?"

"No," I say, turning toward the alley where the two bodies lie in wait, where Ghost showed himself. "Stay away."

"Lilah—"

I hang up and do so with realization. Ghost didn't show himself here, at an Umbrella Man crime scene for no reason. Umbrella Man taunts and kills those close to his victims, but Kane isn't easy to get to. And even if you get to Kane, you won't manipulate him. To get to Kane, you need an expert. An expert like Ghost.

Ghost was telling me that Umbrella Man hired him to kill Kane.

CHAPTER FIVE

There's only one way to win the game.

Play the game.

Some might say winning comes from not playing at all, but in this case, if I don't play, someone else will, and that someone won't do it by choice. They'll also become a victim who will die. I don't plan on going anywhere but to the crime scene to talk to those bodies. And then to the killer's front door, to kick his ass right before killing him. Not a very FBI like thing to say, but fuck it. And fuck it some more.

My phone starts ringing again, and I ignore it. I know it's Kane calling me back. I need to talk to him, considering he left to go battle a cartel controversy, I shouldn't even condone. I am a fucking FBI agent, and Lord help me a part of me really needs to see him right now, but I can't afford that distraction. I can't afford to fear my safety the way he made me fear my safety in that alleyway earlier tonight. I don't know what to do with that. I don't know what to do with him sometimes.

I start walking, ready to step into my Otherworld zone as I do, my place where there is nothing but the crime scene. And it's time, time to read the crime scene. Time to see what's here to see; what Umbrella Man wants me to see. What he thinks I won't see. What he thinks I'm too stupid to see.

"Lilah *fucking* Love."

At Kane's deep, accented, angry voice, I freeze. He's behind me. At the barrier where he just told me he wasn't. And not only is he asking to get a bullet in his head from Ghost, but this breaks our long-standing rule; he doesn't come to my crime scenes or my job. Anger is instant, as is every emotion I feel with this man. I rotate and bring him into view, standing at a wooden barrier a few feet from Brad, and fuck me, he's so damn Kane Mendez. His jacket is gone, his sleeves rolled to his elbows—tall, Latin, and arrogant as fuck. It's like he's daring Umbrella Man and Ghost to come for him. It's like the man thinks he's not fucking human. I want to punch him right now. In fact, he needs to be punched more than anyone I've met tonight, and that's saying a lot.

With more of that award-winning restraint I'm showing tonight, I march toward the line where he stands, and thank fuck, a wooden barrier separates us. It might be the hero who maintains my restraint and the sole reason that I *don't* punch him. "I thought you weren't here, asshole."

"I missed you, too, beautiful." His lips quirk. "As for me being here: obviously, I wasn't, and now I am since you refused to meet me around the corner."

"You didn't come to the barrier and ask for me?"

"No. I did not."

Kane doesn't lie. If he said that he wasn't here until now, he wasn't here until now. "Someone told me I had a visitor, right here at the barrier. That's not a coincidence."

"I'm sure someone did," he says dryly. "And I could give two fucks about that someone. We need to have a conversation we can't have on the phone."

"Later."

"You know me, Lilah, and I know you. If now wasn't necessary, would I be standing here?"

No, no, he would not.

My lips tighten, and I walk around the barrier to step in front of him. He's smart enough not to touch me in front of the live audience, who I can now feel watching us. Fuck them. Really, truly fuck them all. He motions to the wall just beyond the alleyway, and together, we step under the overhang, and I rotate on him.

"What the hell are you doing, Kane? Are you trying to get killed? Ghost showing up here, that was him telling us that Umbrella Man hired him to kill you. And clearly someone knew you were here, not where you said you were, because they told me I had a visitor, You're being watched."

"Ghost and I have an agreement. I pay him double to kill anyone who contracts against me."

"If you're trying to make me feel better, you've forgotten I don't like fluff and bullshit. You think that matters to a man like Ghost?"

"That's all that matters to a man like Ghost."

"What if you're wrong?" I challenge.

"We're back to, you know me. Am I stupid enough to be standing here, or to let you stand here if I didn't believe we were safe?"

"Did you or did you not just try and get me to meet you at the flower shop?"

"Was I supposed to tell you that I have a standing order with a hitman on the phone?"

I open my mouth to say what I've said too often, "You aren't supposed to say that shit to me, ever," but I live with this man now. It's not that simple. The truth is, it's never been that simple. "No. You couldn't say that to me on the phone, and you're right. I needed to know."

His eyes narrow and darken. "That's it?"

"Yes. That's it."

"That's never it for you, Lilah."

"I have two dead bodies and one's a cop, Kane. And the same asshole who killed them, hired Ghost to kill you. The biggest 'fuck you' that I can give this asshole is to catch him, which means I need to be talking to those bodies, not you." I turn away and hesitate, eyeing him again. "That's it *for now.*"

He laughs, low and taunting. I like his laugh, and I will be damned if Umbrella Man is taking it from me. I did a good enough job of that on my own not so long ago. I re-enter the crime scene, and Larry, a brawny cop I know from way back when is now at the barrier. "It's true, then? You're with Kane Mendez?"

I'm not in the mood for this bullshit. "Every fucking night, sometimes twice. Any more questions?" I stop in front of him and arch a brow.

"Ah...no. No more questions."

"Good. Now maybe you can think about who might have killed these two women instead of who I might be fucking. Do we have a name yet for the victim?"

"Not yet."

"I need that fucking name, *now*."

I give him my back and stare at the brightly illuminated alleyway, spotlights beaming down on the crime scene, where tents now cover the bodies that are draped in dark-colored plastic with one thought: why the fuck is Roger here, and leaning over the dead body in the center of the alley? I now have two people to kill: him and Umbrella Man.

CHAPTER SIX

I kneel next to the covered body on the ground, smack in the center of a spotlight illuminating the alleyway, and under a tent. I'm also across from Roger, and I do what I'd once feared: I look directly into his eyes. "What the hell, Roger?" I say. "You can't just show up and start working the case."

"I'd think you'd enjoy my input," he says, his blue eyes as piercing as ever. "You should. I was your mentor. I *am* your mentor."

"Were," I say, and he's right. I should, but I don't, and it has nothing to do with my fear of him looking into my eyes and seeing a killer. I'm here. I'm facing that fear. It's done and gone. Because that's how I roll. I have my moments where I fear what I am and then I have moments where I say "fuck it, I'm a killer, and I don't care who knows." I'm in one of the "fuck it" moments, and for now, that mood isn't going anywhere. "This isn't your case."

"I invited him."

Those words are spoken by Melanie Carmichael, the medical examiner who took over for Beth after I arranged to send her to Europe to get her out of the sights of Umbrella Man. Melanie squats down beside Roger but looks at me. "We were actually talking about this case when I got the call."

I don't need to weigh my reaction, which is decidedly more negative than my more frequent negative reactions. This isn't me being territorial or insecure. I don't need this fucking job. I choose to do it. It's something else. I can feel Roger staring at me, his gaze cutting, his attention unwelcome, and therein lies the problem. This is about the chronic dislike that Roger has started creating in me. Perhaps I never liked him. In fact, I know I didn't, and yet, I wanted to please him. God, I'm fucked up enough to need to drink over this realization, but not before I kill someone;

before I kill Umbrella Man, I amend. I eye Melanie, a pretty black woman I haven't bothered to age until now. She's fifty-something I decide but could pull off forty-something, too young for Roger's sixty-whatever-the-fuck-he-is. And yet, I sense they're together. I sense that it's a new thing, too. But then it could be his mind she's drawn to. He's smart, a keen mind, too smart for most criminals, except this one, or he wouldn't be here right now, asking to be killed.

"While you were talking about Umbrella Man," I say, "he was here with me."

"Because it's personal," Roger says. "You need to let me help before you end up dead."

I eye him. "He won't kill me, not yet, but you, you he'll kill."

A gleam of something pierces those blue eyes before he arches a brow and asks, "And you know this how?"

"Because I know," is the only answer I offer him, "so get up and get the fuck out of here."

"Oh my," Melanie exclaims. "Oh my. Is this why Beth was shipped to Europe. Was she a target? Am I target now, too?"

"No," I say at the same time as Roger, both of us looking at her and then each other.

"You aren't close to Lilah," Roger says, answering for me, holding my stare. "He has no use for you." He leans closer to me. "This case might not even be about you. It could be about me. It could be about my cases. You get that, right? He could want you to get to me. I'm not leaving, and frankly, I'm too old to give a fuck if I live or die."

"And that's why you just told our new medical examiner that he won't go after her?" I challenge. I lean in closer to him. "Because you know, from me reviewing the case with you, that he goes after those close to the victim."

His lips quirk. "You're good, Love. The kind of good worthy of being my protégé."

"What does that mean?" Melanie asks urgently. "Am I in danger or not?"

"No," I say at the same time as Roger again, but neither of us look at her. We look at each other, and the air between us crackles with a challenge. It's not unfamiliar—he was always challenging me—but this is about power and control.

He thinks I'll push back and tell him that I'm in control now, but I learned well. I'm not the one in control nor is he. Umbrella Man is in control and the only way to take that from him is to catch him.

"Roger," Melanie presses urgently.

His lips tighten, a hint of irritation there most wouldn't notice, but I do. I know him. I've studied him for one reason: to be like him, to learn from him. He tears his gaze from mine and reaches over, squeezing her arm. "You're fine." It's the only version of comfort I've ever heard him offer anyone, but then, I've never known him to maintain a romantic interest, which in hindsight is—odd.

He leans in to speak to her, his voice low, for her ears only, and I don't like how distracted she is by him. She needs to be focused on the evidence. His presence has distracted her and me, but it is also starting to rain again. Every second we're in the rain risks evidence being damaged, which, no doubt, Umbrella Man knows.

We need all hands on deck right now, and the truth is, if Umbrella Man gets distracted by Roger, maybe he won't focus on Kane. Which is a really shitty thing for me to think. God. I'm a horrible person. All these realizations about myself seem to come by way of Roger. Maybe that's why I don't like him. While he's looking at me, he's not the one seeing me. I am. I'm seeing me in all the dark and dirty ways that don't turn me on the way they do Kane.

"Lilah?"

I snap back to the moment and eye Roger before I glance at Melanie. "What do you know so far?"

"Nothing," she says. "I literally just arrived. The traffic was horrible and—"

I tune her out, my gaze landing on the victim who needs me right now. She's pretty. She's in her twenties. She's a blonde like the other two victims while I'm brunette. That fact has stuck out to me and stuck with me. I'm not like them. He believes I'm like him. He believes, like Ghost, that I'm another killer. I hope he does think I'm like him. I hope he underestimates me because I'm not the killer he believes I am. I'm the killer I know I am. She's someone that no one fully understands, not even me yet, but my gut says we're going to meet her before this is over, and we all hope she's a bitch.

CHAPTER SEVEN

People rambling generally piss me off, like now.

Melanie and Roger launch into a conversation about the rain and the impact on the body, Forensics 101, which doesn't matter right now. The damn body is covered in plastic because that's how this asshole made sure this woman left this alleyway and this world. Wrapped in fucking *plastic*. I'm going to wrap his ass in plastic and that means I can't keep listening to these two rambling. I need to be in my own world, my Otherworld.

Blocking out more Forensics 101, I squeeze my eyes shut and go there now. *Fuck Roger.* He won't be the reason I miss something I can't afford to miss. And *Fuck Umbrella Man.* If he wants a me versus him showdown, a one-on-one matchup, he's got it. I'm more committed than ever.

Me versus him. I mentally replay it again.

In this scenario, the hit on Kane doesn't add up. Umbrella Man goes after the victim's loved ones. If I'm not a victim, if I'm like him, why go after Kane? It could be a head game. It could be him trying to push my limits or distract me from what's right in front of my face. And what is it that's right in *front* of my face?

I open my eyes and stare down at what amounts to a tarp over the body, replaying what I know. Three victims who died holding umbrellas. There's Williams, too, and the family members of the victims, but staying focused on the core crimes, there are three victims holding umbrellas.

All blonde.

One was a natural blonde. One was a bleached blonde. I tied that to myself the only way I can. In her most iconic role, my mother dyed her hair blonde to play Marilyn Monroe. Anyone who knows who I am, who does any digging at all, would tie me to her. She won awards. She was on billboards. It's not a far reach, especially if Umbrella Man is testing my skills and wants to make me work for my answers.

I pull on gloves, grab my flashlight, and lift the plastic, scanning her face; there's makeup smudged on it, clown-like when Umbrella Man is a man of perfection. He's anal. He's perfect. That doesn't add up.

I check the hair and find brown roots, which makes her a brunette like me. Her hair is bleached. Next, I yank the plastic higher to expose her hands, with the gun and umbrella taped in them.

"They wanted to take the weapon because it was loaded, but I insisted they leave it," Melanie says. "They removed the bullets."

My gaze jerks to hers, and I lower the plastic.

"There are insights I might lose should they move her before I'm done," she adds.

I give her a deadpan look and try to bite my tongue. No. No, actually, I don't try at all. "Now I know why Umbrella Man wanted Beth gone," I say. "Beth doesn't teach class. Beth doesn't suck. She solves the crime. Solve the fucking crime. And don't talk to the press to hear yourself talk some more."

She looks stunned, the kind of stunned that makes you think the person just had a stick stuck up her ass. God, what I wouldn't do for a stick to carry around this crime scene right now. "Talking to the press will piss me off," I add. "To clarify what that means, right now, this ranks as only mildly irritated." I eye Roger, who also likes to hear himself talk. Maybe they're a match made in heaven and Lord help us all. "That means you, too. No press."

I don't give him time to reply.

I push to my feet and shove my flashlight in my pocket.

"They were all right," Melanie says. "You're a bitch."

"I prefer Dark Knight," I say, dryly. "You know, like Batman. And really, he's kind of a bitch, too, though I think he looks better in the costume than me. I'll have to work on that." I shrug. "Or not." And with that, I step into the downpour of rain, tuning her out, tuning everyone out, but the two women and their killer. My hood protects me from the rain's punishment. The tents protect the bodies from the same, but I wonder how much evidence was washed away before they were in place. I walk to the second tent, to Detective Williams' new safe place, if you can call it that, where a CSI guy is shooting photos of the ground near the now covered body, working the area. I know that he's CSI because of his jacket and a vague memory that places him at the NYPD in my past life.

"Anything worth noting?" I ask, pulling down my hood.

His look is grim, his jaw stubbled a salt and pepper shadow, his age mid-forties. His green eyes notably pale. I don't know his name, or him. I'd remember those eyes. "Mitch McAllen," he says as if seeing the question in my face. "And the rain's a bitch, Agent Love, but I'm trying to get you something to get this bastard."

In another time and place, I'd ask for a moment alone with the body. It's my thing. When I can get the time to have a little conversation with the dead myself, I take it, but today is not that day. Not on the timeline that the rain and wind, that is now gusting into the tent, creates. I pull my hood back up and motion him into action. "Keep going. Keep looking."

He gives a nod, his demeanor calm and calculated, his energy the same. He's easy to tune out, and I do just that. I tune him out. I don't, however, immediately step to the body. I think of the rain and how messy it all feels, but in reality, it's water, and water is clean. Based on the immaculate crime scenes we've seen to date, he likes clean. Though pigs' blood from a ceiling fan isn't exactly clean. It's filled with pathogens that a person who is clearly OCD wouldn't appreciate.

Unless—the person isn't OCD at all.

Maybe Umbrella Man is simply a control freak who enjoys making people do something uncomfortable and hard. And cleaning to absolute perfection while fearing for your life, or perhaps a limb, fits that mold. Expanding the suspect list to control freaks also prevents an overly narrow suspect list. It's a premise to take to Purgatory with me when I finally have the chance.

I walk to the body, and the bright lights that CSI have shining down on the tarp at the moment make my flashlight unnecessary. I pull back the tarp, uncovering Detective

Williams from the waist up, for my first one-on-one with her since she muddied up the crime scene several nights back, quite literally. She'd shown zero signs of OCD or that of a control freak. A control freak would want a crime scene done her way and right. And yet, a pretty redhead in her mid-forties doesn't fit the victims either. She's not him. She's not one of them. What am I missing?

"Love."

At Houston's voice, I pull the tarp back into place and turn to greet him. "We have a name and address for the victim." His look is grim, hesitant even. There's something more, something he doesn't think I want to hear.

"What? Say it. This isn't my first, tenth, or one-hundredth rodeo."

He pulls down his hood and fixes me with a piercing stare. "She lives in Kane's building, Lilah. That means your building."

That sinks in nice and slow, kind of like the way a brutal hot sauce set in your mouth feels like it's burning holes in your tongue. Umbrella Man thinks he has Ghost. He thinks we don't know he has Ghost. Therefore, his message is a promise to me that he can get to Kane.

CHAPTER EIGHT

Umbrella Man came at me like a Pitbull in ballerina shoes, waltzing in right under my nose, with teeth bared and ready to rip out Kane's throat. He underestimates me and Kane if he believes that's going to happen. He won't get Kane. He won't get me. He won't even so much as stir an emotional reaction in me, not here, not now, none that he will ever know exists. I focus on what matters right now, the ticking clock. "What about the victim's family?" I ask because no matter how hard Umbrella Man is coming at me, I can fight. I can win. The family might not.

"Her only living family here is her mother, who is lucky as fuck to be in Europe right now, where she's likely safer. Of course, I know, I get it—one of the victim's parents died while they were supposed to be on a cruise, but I'd like to think Europe helps. Her twin sister lives in California. I've reached out to those officials for safety checks."

"And the victim's apartment?"

"I've sent a team to discreetly secure it until you give further directions. An additional CSI team is also on the way, along with an additional ten men. That's all I can spare right now. Sergeant Morris is in charge; he's a good man."

"Who was fucking Williams," I say, pulling off my gloves. "Get me someone else. He's a person of interest."

He blanches. "What?"

"Out of his mouth to my ears but he can say otherwise. Well, he said he dated her. He didn't admit to doing kinky shit to her, but that goes without saying."

"He's already on-site, and he's a good man, Lilah."

"So, she must have said. He can stay. Umbrella Man didn't leave anything behind he doesn't want me to find, and I want to observe him." I move on. "Name, age, occupation of the victim?"

"Morris is the best man out here," he says. "He didn't kill Williams or anyone else."

"They said that about Jeffrey Dahmer, too. Name, age—
"

"Karen Nicole White," he bites out. "Twenty-eight. Soap opera star. A one-way ticket to lots of press."

He's right, and that, of course, was not an accident, any more than her home address was.

I shove the gloves in a plastic bag, working the data as Houston gives it to me, but my mind races beyond that information. Umbrella Man wants me to go to Kane. He wants me to worry about Kane. Maybe he expects Ghost to kill Kane tonight in our own building. No. That's not his plan. The victim would be my warning. He wants us to think we can stop him. He'll want me to believe that I can protect Kane while he believes I can't.

Kane can protect fucking Kane. He doesn't seem to get that.

And if I want to call Kane, I'll fucking call Kane.

I pull my phone from my pocket, turning away from Houston, intent on calling Kane, only to have Houston grab my arm. This is twice he's touched me, and I don't like being touched. It's all I can do not to whirl on him and react fiercely, but I have no doubt that I'm being watched. And I will not show weakness. "Why is your hand on my arm?" I ask softly, my voice low, tight.

"What are you about to do right now?"

"Why is that your business?" I challenge.

"You're too close to this to be objective," he says. "You can't work this case."

I give him a tiny smile and calmly say, "Get your hand off my arm, Houston, before I rip it off."

He must read how much I might enjoy that because his hand falls away and fast like it's already yanked off and near bleeding. "You're going to end up dead, Lilah. You know that, right?"

I think of him showing up here when he shouldn't have been able to get here that fast. "Is that a threat?"

He scowls. "What the fuck does that even mean?"

"Umbrella Man wants me on this case," I say. "I'm on this case."

"And you think giving him what he wants is smart?"

"This isn't about what he wants," I say. "It's about what I want. And I want him."

"You can't be objective," he says. "There's no fucking way at this point you can be objective."

"I don't need to be objective. I just need to be right. And when I'm right, he's *dead*."

"Is there a problem?" Roger asks, stepping to our profiles.

"You can't kill him," Houston says, ignoring Roger. "And if that's where this is going—"

"It is," I assure him, a warning to him if he's Umbrella Man. "He'll be dead before this is over. Because that's what he wants."

"He wants to die?" Houston laughs. "You're losing your fucking mind."

"That happened several years back," I assure him. "It works for me. You should give it a try. Maybe then you'd stop running from the mayor and your own shadow." With that, I turn away, but I don't make it far without yet another opinion I don't want flying at me anyway.

"I agree," Roger calls after me. "One of you dies before this is over."

Those words have a different impact coming from him than they had me. They stop me in my tracks and proceed to crawl down my spine and back up again, but I don't turn to face Roger. I'm too busy trying to read my reaction, but I don't get the chance before he adds, "Maybe you should ask for help before it's you."

Ah, there it is. The reason I react to his statement so fucking badly. I knew where he was going. I knew it was right here where we're at, to me being too stupid to stay alive. I rotate and face him. "You never did get me, Roger." It's a statement just a week ago I'd fear because, getting me, means seeing what I'm capable of, getting me, means seeing that I'm far more like the bad guys we hunt than I should be to wear this badge. "If you did, you'd know that I'm not the one who dies in this story." I eye Houston. "I need an update on the wellness check the minute you have it. Get the family into protective custody if you can." I scan for the CSI guy who is shooting a photo of the same spot he was shooting earlier. Can I get no one here who knows what the fuck they're doing? I glance at Houston again. "Make sure he's not part of the new CSI team."

"Agent Love," he bites out, "on the record, you don't belong on this case. I'm taking that to your superior."

"And Director Murphy will tell you what I'm telling you right now: fuck off, Houston. He'll just say it in more formal, less offensive language. I don't think he likes the word 'fuck' all that much, a character flaw, I know, but he'll get the point across."

With that, I turn away from him, and this time, I step out from underneath the tent, the way I have the shadow of fear I'd associated with Roger. It's an odd thing, really, that I even let it exist. Fear, like the bullshit Houston is pulling, isn't my thing. I push through the punishing rain and pull my phone from my pocket, dialing Kane. He answers on the first ring. "Lilah."

"Karen Nicole White. Soap opera star who lives in our building. Do you know her?"

"I know *of* her. I had everyone in the building investigated. What's going on, Lilah?"

"She's the dead woman lying in the alley."

He's silent a moment. "And so, this is war?"

"Yes," I say. "And so, this is war. Meet me in front of our building. Let's tell him to fuck off together."

"I do like how you think, Lilah Love."

CHAPTER NINE

The walk to the building I now live in with Kane is short, and rain battered from the aftermath of a bitch of a late-season hurricane. I reach the building to find a barrier around the entryway, and officers guarding entry. Kane isn't here yet. I flash my badge to the officer guarding the walkway setup to the door, between barriers. "Agent Love," I say. "Are you allowing tenants into the building?"

"That was my direction," Sergeant Morris says, exiting the building to join us, almost as if he's daring me to send him away. "Tenants only, by way of the security desk, but the elevators are down. No one is going up or down right now. I just sent the team up by foot. They'll call down as soon as the apartment is secure."

"I'd send you to Detective Williams' building to check things out, but we've both already been there." It's an attempt to push his buttons, and it works.

His eyes burn fire. "You think you're funny?" he asks. "Because I don't think it's fucking funny."

"Ohhh, bad words. You really don't think it's funny. But neither do I. That wasn't a joke. And while telling a good joke might, to some, seem like my superpower, it's not. Catching killers. That's my superpower."

"Lilah."

At the sound of Kane's voice, I add, "Let me know the minute you have word on the apartment or the family." With that, I walk toward the barrier.

"You need a new superpower," Morris calls after me.

I ignore him. I find ignoring people works in several ways. A) It makes them mad. B) It makes them act out. And when people act out, they often show you just a little bit of the real stuff they hide underneath all their fluff. And everyone has fluff. I hate fluff. Besides, of course, he wants me to find a new superpower. I'm giving him attention that he doesn't want.

I exit the barrier and walk to the left, under an overhang, where Kane is waiting, not a damp hair on his pretty little head. Kit, the big burly guard who is usually at the front desk of the building, is by his side, which tells me he's under Kane's employ and far more than a staffer here at the property. That Kane is keeping him close also tells me that Kane isn't taking the threat as lightly as he will play it off. I give Kit a wave, and in silent understanding, Kane and I move further down the walkway, with Kit between us and the front door. We're now in a listen-in-free zone, free of any potential microphones or overly attentive eyes.

"It's a new day when you invite me to your crime scene," Kane comments dryly.

"It's a fucked up day when that crime scene is in the building we now live in together," I say, stepping in front of him and pulling down my hood. "And I work for Murphy now, who doesn't want me for my body or skill; he wants me for my crime lord lover."

"I'll respond to the many things wrong with that reply when we're finally *alone*."

"You'll get over whatever pissed you off by the time we're finally alone, so whatever," I say. "I have to go upstairs and walk her damn apartment. Where, he's, of course, left me some sort of message, but," I lower my voice, "we're assuming that he still thinks that Ghost is going to kill you, but Ghost killed those women in the alleyway to keep the booby traps from killing me. Which wouldn't have killed me because Umbrella Man was not ready to have me killed."

"And you're afraid that he saw Ghost kill them to protect you," he says, following my lead, "and no longer believes he's going to kill me."

"Or maybe he paid Ghost to kill them." My eyes go wide. "Fuck. Fuck. *Fuck*. That's it. He paid Ghost to kill them. This is one big fucked up game, and Kane, I'm not sure you really have Ghost handled."

"I am," he says. "That's what matters."

"No, that is not what fucking matters. I'm the one who has to bury you if you die, asshole." I've started poking his chest. Good lord, help me. I drop my hands. "We'll *talk* later."

His lips quirk. "Yes. We'll *talk* later."

"He didn't come here to warn you, asshole. He came here to save me because he was paid to save me."

"I have an agreement with Ghost. *Trust me,* even if you don't trust him."

An unwelcomed memory of me sitting in a bathroom wearing bloodied clothes with him standing above me punches at my mind. I'm pretty sure at that point there was a body in his trunk. A body that has never been found. "What if you're wrong?" I ask.

"I just got you back, Lilah." His eyes darken. "And you're the only thing that keeps me human, as proven in ways you can't begin to understand the past twenty-four hours. I need you too damn much to lose you."

I don't ask what that means. Not now. Maybe not ever. "Then don't take risks."

"I wouldn't risk anything that ends in losing you."

"What about me losing you?"

"Same thing. Do your job. Catch him. I'll back up your team and secure the building behind them."

I nod, and we rejoin Kit. "I need to see the security footage, starting with the last time Karen was seen."

"Two days ago," he says. "I already looked. She left. Her sister arrived four hours later."

Now he has my attention. "Her sister?"

"Said she was in for a visit. She came in and out of the apartment several times. She's up there now."

"Agent Love."

At the sound of my name, I go cold because I know what I'm about to be told. I turn to find Sergeant Morris standing at the barrier nearest me, his expression grim. "There's another body."

"Yes," he says. "Another woman. Shot to death. Possible suicide."

"It's not a fucking suicide," I snap.

His lips thin. "I know who she is," he says. "I can identify the body."

Of course, he can, but I don't need his help. I already know who she is. "It's her twin sister," I say.

"Yes," he confirms. "It's her sister."

And the reason she was killed here, in this building, is pretty fucking obvious. It was one thing to kill someone who lived here, outside in the alleyway. Another to kill someone inside the building where I live. Where Kane lives. Umbrella Man is telling us that our fortress is not impenetrable.

CHAPTER TEN

This is war.

Kane said it.

I endorse his position enthusiastically.

I don't, however, offer Sergeant Morris some big, over the top reaction. He's not Umbrella Man. Williams wasn't Umbrella Man. But I don't know if they are somehow involved with Umbrella Man. It's an odd place for my thoughts to travel in the first place, but my mind is going where it wants to go, without my permission.

And so, I simply ask, "What about an update on the mother?"

"Nothing yet," Morris replies.

"I'll be right up, " I reply, a clear dismissal in the statement.

Surprise flickers in his eyes. "You aren't going to tell me to leave?"

"I'm not done with you," I say. "So no. I'm not going to tell you to leave."

He inclines his chin, remarkably and uncomfortably compliant, which I'd like to think is about shock and grief, but he was belligerent only an hour ago. That makes this a hard sell now.

Kane steps to my side. "You don't like him."

"He ranks right up there with mushrooms for me."

"That's some pretty serious hate."

"Yes," I say. "Yes, it is."

"He didn't get past security," he says. "The sister killed herself."

"To save her twin." I glance up at him. "That's how he works. He plays with the family members and then convinces them to shoot 1 themselves because a bullet is simply nothing to him. Because they are nothing to him. They're inconsequential."

"You understand him. You'll get him. Stop letting him fuck with your head."

"He's trying," I agree, "but it's not working."

He turns to face me and me him. "You sure about that?"

"You doubt me?"

"Never. But clearly you doubt me."

"You think you're bulletproof. You're human."

His lips quirk. "You worry about me."

"I do fucking worry about you, asshole. Stop throwing it in my face." I start to turn away but stop, facing him again. "If you come face-to-face with him, I don't care what trap he says he set for me, you kill him." I grab his tie and yank it. "Understand?"

"And if he threatens me, will you do what you have to do, and kill him? Or will you be suckered into thinking that you can save me?"

The idea of him dead punches me in the chest and I hesitate. Fuck. I hesitate. "I'll kill him so dead, there won't be any of him left."

"I don't believe you," he says, "but I have faith in your ability to remedy that weakness."

"Bastard," I murmur, releasing my grip on his tie. "Let's go." I don't give him time to agree. I turn and walk through the barriers, and he's right there with me, as is Kit. I don't bother to clear either with the officer by the door. Kit is employed here, and Kane is Kane. He lives here.

I enter the building and hear, "Love."

At Houston's voice, I turn to find him entering the building. He scrubs his jaw. "The mother's dead, too," he says, stopping in front of me. "Shot herself in a Paris hotel room. And the press is everywhere. I just talked to the mayor. He wants to hold a press conference."

"This again?" I breathe out. "He needs to wait."

"This building drips money and power. We need to calm the residents, two of which called the press."

"She killed herself. It's a suicide."

"She's in an alleyway," he argues.

"I don't have time for this, Houston. I need to be upstairs, looking at the evidence."

"This is happening, whether you deal with it or not."

My lips press together. "Stand up to the mayor."

"You tried that. How'd that go for you?"

"You're a coward."

"Fuck you, Lilah."

"No thanks, but try that with the mayor. No press conference. This is my case. This is my call."

"And *his* city."

"I thought it was yours. Oh right, you're his little bitch, so what is yours, is his. Maybe I should get you one of those submissive choker necklaces. If you wear that then everyone will just ask you, who's your Master, and you can say the mayor. And you can then explain that you have no safeword. The mayor never stops making the decisions."

"Are you done?"

"Never really done. Haven't you figured that out?"

"Most of us have."

"Good," I say, but I want to hit him. I want to go to the mayor's house and hit him, too. I want to dress them up like the clowns they are and then hit them. "You want to hold a press conference," I say, "then you tell the city that you're investigating what may be a double suicide." I turn and start walking away, but I turn and walk backward. "The only conflict of interest going on is you and the mayor trying to cover your asses to keep your jobs." I turn and walk to the stairwell, opening the door and entering the corridor.

I start the fifteen floor climb up the stairs, only two floors beneath our level, anger burning into calm, as I force myself to find that Otherworld. I need my zone. I need to focus. I'm there, thinking about the case. I need—the lights go out. I curse in my mind, but not out of my mouth. Instinct has me reaching for my weapon. Once it's in my palm, a heavy bump of comforting weight, I reach for my flashlight. I'm about to turn it on when a door several feet above opens and then shuts. No light comes on. I would assume that means someone without a flashlight exited to the hallway, but there's one problem with that theory: no one but law enforcement would be in the stairwell right now. I'm once again in the darkness, and I'm not alone.

CHAPTER ELEVEN

A couple of dead bodies.

A storm.

Elevator broken.

Empty stairwell.

Girl alone in a stairwell.

Lights out.

I'm officially living a B horror flick, only someone screwed up and gave the chick, who's alone in the dark stairwell, a gun. Correction. Someone screwed up and gave the crazy-as- fuck chick, who will shoot your ass, a gun. This realization, that I'm that chick, is pretty darn comforting right now. Because I will shoot your ass. I will shoot whoever is in this stairwell with me. Well, unless it's someone I like, and that list isn't long. I consider my options and decide that whoever is in here with me, is trying to scare me, which means, it's Umbrella Man. This news isn't terrifying at all. He's fucking with me, as Kane said a few minutes earlier, which means he's not done with me. He's not going to shoot me the minute he hears my steps.

With that in mind, I start feeling for steps and inching my way upward. One step, two, five, ten. I make it to another level and repeat, stopping to listen in between my upward movement, hearing nothing but then I'm a stealthy bitch. I know my visitor can't hear me either. In other words, silence doesn't equal absence. Two flights up, I sense his nearness, and I want this done—perhaps I'm not so patient after all. I flip on my flashlight and rush forward. In the same moment, or perhaps a moment later, another flashlight comes on, and in a split second, I'm on a landing, facing off, gun to flashlight, with a tall, big man. A familiar man.

"What the fuck Sergeant Morris?" I demand. "What is this?"

"What the fuck is right," he growls. "No one is supposed to be in here unless they clear it through me first. Use the radio." He curses under his breath and lowers his weapon. "The last thing I need is you thinking that I'm trying to kill you, too. I setup a procedure, and Agent in Charge or whatever the fuck you are, you still have to follow it or end up getting fired on."

I don't lower my weapon. "What fucking radio? Houston didn't tell me about a radio."

"I didn't even know Houston was in the building. I have a point man downstairs."

"Well, he failed miserably. Why the hell are the lights out?"

"I'm on my way to the utility room now, but in case you didn't notice, there's damn near a hurricane outside."

"This is a high-end building. I guarantee there's a backup generator."

There's a slight sound, a barely-there echo that has me turning and standing next to Morris, both of us raising our weapons and pointing. Seconds tick by while we both wait for what comes next. And then the lights flicker and turn back on. A door somewhere several floors down opens and then shuts. We weren't alone but that doesn't change my opinion of Sergeant Morris. It doesn't change my opinion of Williams. Something with the two of them just doesn't add up.

The door opens again. "Morris! You in here? Agent Love? Everyone okay in there?"

Morris relaxes. "Yes, Nick. We're good."

"Maintenance guy got the generator going," the man calls out. "It was a lightning strike that threw out the power."

I don't know if I buy that, but I lower my weapon. I don't, however, put it away.

Sergeant Morris turns to me and eyes my weapon, harnessing his with exaggerated precision. "You going to shoot me, or should I escort you to the crime scene?"

"Walk," I order, motioning him toward the stairs. "You first."

His jaw flexes. "You trust me that much, huh?"

"I trust you not at all."

"But I need to trust you and give you my back?"

"That about sums it up. So hurry the fuck up the stairs. I have a dead body waiting on me that isn't yours. Yet."

He shakes his head in evident disgust, but he starts walking. I eye the stairwell beneath us, even going so far as to lean over the railing to confirm that no one is following me before I fall into step behind him. Three floors later, he opens the door, and when he holds the door for me, I grimace. "Really?"

"Whatever, Agent Love," he says, walking ahead of me and exiting to the hallway.

Then, and only then, do I holster my weapon while Morris speaks to someone over his damn radio. Where the hell was his point man when I came upstairs? I catch the door and exit to the hallway to find him waiting on me. "I need to follow up on the power outage," he says, motioning around the corner. "You'll find the apartment secure." His lips thin, and he just stands there.

"Say whatever the fuck you need to say because it's taken me way too long to get to that body."

"That's not her apartment."

My brows furrow. "Then who the fuck's apartment is it? Did she have a sugar daddy?"

He scowls. "No, she didn't have a sugar daddy. What the hell, Agent Love?"

"What the hell, exactly. Who the hell does the apartment belong to?"

"It's hers, it's just not hers." He shifts his weight from one foot to the other.

Then a realization hits me. "You knew the victim?"

"She's one of Detective Williams' sorority sisters. Both of the twins were. They were all close."

"And you know this because you weren't fucking Williams?"

"I told you. We dated. We had dinner here a few times." He grimaces and presses his hands to his hips. "My point is," he continues, "that I was here. I saw the apartment. Karen lived in chaos. That apartment is not chaos. It's like someone else lived there."

He means it's been turned into an OCD field of dreams, which means, somehow, Umbrella Man made that happen here, in this building. We've just determined that he was here, in this building. We've determined he might have been jealous enough to target Ralph Redman, Williams' recent boyfriend. I should be celebrating cornering a killer, but it's too easy.

"She was messy as hell," he rambles on. "Just like Detective Williams. That was a problem for us. I like clean and neat. I'm a bit anal that way. She's not. She's wasn't. She was a slob." He cuts his stare, seeming to choke up before he looks at me. "That apartment, Karen's apartment, now looks like mine. Perfect. She didn't keep her apartment like this. She didn't." He scrubs his jaw. Again. "Me being a neat freak doesn't mean I did this. I didn't have to tell you that. You wouldn't know I was ever here."

"There are cameras in the building," I remind him. "Maybe you were preempting me seeing you in the feed. Or preparing me for what I'd find in your apartment should I search it."

"I could just mess my apartment up."

He could, but extreme OCD might make him feel he was better off explaining his neatness.

"I didn't kill her," he says.

"*I* didn't kill her," I say. "And that's the only statement I consider true right now. What's the sister's name?"

"Katy."

"Tell me about Katy," I order.

"I didn't meet her, but Karen said that she's a model and an aspiring actress. That's why she moved to LA last year. To act."

And there it is, the missing piece of the puzzle.

Now I have the connection between Detective Williams and the other victims.

Holy fuck.

The obvious just hit me. Why the hell it took me this long I don't know. This isn't all about Williams. She's not even the main victim. She's the "family member," in this case, the sister, and I use that term lightly, who lured me into that alleyway to save her sorority sister. Umbrella Man chose a circle of friends who complement one goal. He's drawing me a picture of blood and death.

The posed, primary victims include two models, one of which was retired and in advertising, a literary agent, and an actress, all involved in the media. They all live in the world my mother inhabited. They connect to me by way of my mother's stardom, her career.

This isn't me solving his random crimes. This is him killing on my behalf, because of me. Maybe even killing *for me.*

CHAPTER TWELVE

He thinks he's perfect.

That's what the whole OCD clean is all about. I'm not sure he's actually OCD. I think it's more about him telling me he's perfect, he's unbeatable. He just doesn't know how fucking perfect a slob like me can be, but he'll find out.

"Agent Love," Sergeant Morris says, "I want—"

"And that's your problem," I snap. "This is still about you. You want. That, and you talk way too fucking much." I step around him because really, truly, he's not the guy. He's not the killer. He might, in fact, be another victim who actually lived.

I stop walking and turn around. He steps around the corner to face me. I close the space between me and him. "Were you being blackmailed by the killer?" He blanches. "What? No. Hell no. What are you even talking about?"

"Have you been into the apartment?"

"You know I have. I just told you, it's cleaned up."

"Did you look at the body?"

"No." His lips thin. "I heard—I heard it's—"

"Bloody?"

"Yes," he confirms.

"You don't like blood," I accuse.

"No one likes blood," he says.

I sure as fuck don't, I think, but what I say is, "He does. The killer likes it a lot. He likes that you don't even more. Every one of his victims has someone close to them blackmailed and then killed. Williams was the one who got blackmailed over her sister. Everyone who is blackmailed is now dead. He kills them. In other words, if you're lying to me—"

"I'm not lying," he snaps.

"A lie is a death sentence." I shrug. "But I warned you. I'm done." I turn and start walking.

65

"She had a plan. She wouldn't have traded you for her sister."

I stop walking, but I don't turn. I don't say a word. He's right. She wouldn't have. Because Umbrella Man's not ready for me to die. He clearly was ready for Katy and Karen to die. God, even the names are similar, twins and all.

I round the corner, leaving him behind with finality this time, heading toward the apartment where Karen lived and Katy died. That's the new battlefield, and that's where I win. That's where Mr. Perfect Umbrella Man made a mistake. I just have to find it.

The crime scene is my purpose right now, and I don't believe Morris killed anyone. I also don't believe he's telling me the entire truth. I'm not sure yet what that means, but I will. Right now, it's me and Katy. No. It's me and Umbrella Man. My gloves are on by the time I'm at the door.

"Agent Love. Who's inside?" I shrug out of my cumbersome rain jacket and drop it to the floor.

"No one," the twenty-something cop informs me. "I was told once the scene was secure to hold it for you. Not even CSI gets in."

"At whose direction?"

"Chief Houston."

He doesn't want me involved, but he held the scene for me. Houston's a clusterfuck of contradictions these days.

"It's messy in there," the officer adds. "I was told to tell you they contained the mess in the bedroom by turning off the ceiling fan."

Because it's raining blood again. Of course, it is. He had to create a similar death for both sisters. "Who is 'they'?" I ask.

"The officers who were first on the scene."

"Where are they now?"

He stands a little straighter. "Throwing up." He clears his throat. "Both of them."

At least he's honest. "Morning sickness will do that to you."

"No, they—" he stops and laughs nervously, "That was a joke."

66

"Why yes," I say, pulling on a pair of booties I've retrieved from my bag. "It was. I was calling them—"

"Girls," he supplies. "That's not all that politically correct."

Now, he's irritating me. "Why the fuck do I want to be politically correct? Tell them if they fight like girls, too, to go home." I open the apartment door and step inside, entering my Otherworld, and shutting myself inside it and the luxury apartment. I turn and take it in. It's small but beautiful, the living room area cozy and intimate. I do what I do and that means I don't rush to the main blood and gore. I take my time and ensure I miss nothing. And so, I slowly tick off my observations, looking for something that stands out. The floors are a pale tan wood. The couches cream-colored. One large oval window in the center of the room. There's a fireplace with bookshelves filled with books and trinkets, most from movies and television shows. Every book is lined up and measured to perfection.

I walk to the shelf and run a finger over the wood. Not a hint of dust. Stepping to the center of the room, I stare at the perfect square that the blanket is folded into. I eye the pillows set on each side of the couch at the exact same angle. Katy did this. I have no doubt of this. He made all the family members clean to perfection as one of their duties to save their loved ones. And I now know that she was that family member, trying to save her sister.

But how did he inspect her work?

He could have been here, and obviously, I could go back to Morris as a suspect, but it's not him. So was the real killer here? I pull my phone from my pocket and dial my trusty tech guy, Tic Tac. "Lilah."

"I'm living with Kane."

"Oh ah—like the crime lord?"

"He's not a crime lord, asshole."

"That's not what I heard."

"Stop talking and listen before you make me force our boss to relocate you here."

"You can't force Director Murphy to do that."

"Don't take risks you can't afford to live with," I say. "Take notes. I need the security footage for this building for the past thirty days."

"Don't date that dangerous man if you think he's fucking around on you."

"Holy fuck, Tic Tac. I have a dead body. The soap opera star on the fifteenth floor. I need to know if the security footage covers private floors."

"Oh. Crap. Yeah. Okay. I'll look now."

"Just text me. I have a body to talk to right now."

"I hate when you say things like that."

I hang up. I need to focus. And as much as I want to walk the rest of the apartment now, CSI will be here any second. I want just a few minutes with Katy on my own. I follow the hallway that leads to the rest of the apartment and find crime scene tape in front of the bedroom door. I inhale and let it out. I know what's inside this room. It's nothing I can't handle, but this has become personal. This killer knows me far more than I know him. He knows at least one of my weaknesses, and that's Kane. The other is blood, buckets of blood. Damn it, I'm afraid that's what I'm about to find in this room, and it pisses me off that I'm letting him get to me. He will not get to me. Fuck Umbrella Man. Fuck him ten ways to Sunday. I will fuck him up. He doesn't get to fuck me up. Holy hell, just give me an umbrella and a few minutes alone with him, and I will make him walk funny for the rest of his life.

I step inside the damn room.

CHAPTER THIRTEEN

I forget my own anxiety the minute I'm actually inside the victim's bedroom. I step into my Otherworld, really step into it, and everything else slides away. Of course, it helps that there are no puddles of blood waiting for me in the bedroom.

There is just Katy. Ready to tell me a story I need to hear.

She's in the center of the bed, an umbrella taped to her hand, her arm over her head.

Dead.

Naked.

Covered in the same splattered blood that blots the white bedspread and white walls. I now believe the bedspread, which seems to be an exact match to the one in the prior victim's house, to have been brought in for the occasion, for contrasting effect, of course. All of this is about an impact statement. I file that away in my mind as a possible mistake. They were purchased. They can be traced.

My gaze returns to the victim, to Katy. That she's on the bed, and not the floor, as was the prior victim, is interesting. It might appear to be a gentler ending to some, even to him, but it's not, not to me. She's still dead. She's still a body with a name attached that no longer matters, at least not to her. It is, however, no accident. It's a message that I'm supposed to read and understand. I don't have two flips of an idea, right now, what that means. Maybe it's simply supposed to make me hyperfocus and miss something bigger. Maybe it's a test.

Last time, he left me a clue with the cigarettes, Roger's cigarette brand, which still seems to indicate this matchup between him and me connects to an old case that I worked under Roger. Yes, it could be about Roger; *Roger*, I think, hearing his comments from earlier in my head, but it's not. And that we're here, at my building, is a message to me about me, in the building I was always at when I worked for the NYPD because I was engaged to Kane.

Engaged.

Fuck that took me to a place that isn't in my zone.

"Fuck you, Kane Mendez, for distracting me," I murmur and refocus on the damn room.

There's a clue here for me. I need to find it before the team gets here, and, somehow, it's misplaced. I scan the blood patterns on the wall, studying them, looking for patterns but find nothing this time when the patterns led me to the cigarettes last time. It would be too simple for him to leave a clue the same way he did before. I walk to the body and stare down at the white foam on Katy's red-painted lips. She was poisoned. She was wearing lipstick. For him? Because he made her? Because she wanted to please him? Did the sick fuck watch her undress? I think yes. He was here. He had to be here when she died, and undressing her after she died, touching her, would come with the risk of leaving behind DNA.

He could get her to undress by phone or video, which could be traced, but how would he poison her? I look around for a glass or food, but there's nothing. He's too perfectly clean for a dirty glass to sit out. I'm betting if I go to the kitchen, there isn't a glass there either, but she's posed. He was here. If he convinced her to poison herself, she would have thrashed around in pain like the victim in the alleyway I tried to save. She would not be laid out like she was modeling. Coming here was living dangerously. He knows someone saw him. They had to have seen him. That means I can find that someone. He's daring me to find someone who saw him. He's daring me to find him.

And so, I will.

Where are her clothes?

I walk to the closet and open the door to find a silver dress on the floor. I pull out my camera and take a few photos and then my gaze lifts to the poster on the wall. It's the band U2 with the song title "With or Without You" on it, the words to the song written out in the shape of a guitar. It's as if the room goes wide and shrinks again, a memory from my past surfacing. There are voices in the apartment, the CSI team arriving. My gaze lands on a verse: *You give it all but I want more.*

Suddenly, I'm flashing back to the Hamptons, to the night I was raped. I was at a bar with my then best friend, Alexandra. She'd insisted we drink the champagne she'd ordered. I remember that champagne because it was my birthday and it's all I drank that night. She was off flirting with a man, and Kane had just texted. He was flying home early. I was eager to meet him. I paid the bill, but I was suddenly quite dizzy. I stepped outside to the parking lot.

The cold night air of the parking lot helps me breathe, but something's not right. I don't feel right. I walk toward my car, but I sway again, a wave of confusion taking hold. I reach the driver's side of my BMW, or what I think is my BMW. Whatever the case, I catch myself on the hard steel. I'm losing reality. I'm fading, and some part of my mind knows that I've been drugged and that I need to get in the car and lock the doors. And help. I need to call for help.

I shove my hand into my pocket, digging for my keys, and my fingers touch the cold steel, but I can't seem to grip it. I lower my head to the side of the car, drawing in a deep breath, trying to calm myself down. It doesn't help. There are sounds behind me. Voices. Laughter. "Alexandra?" I whisper, certain I hear her, but she doesn't reply. "Alexandra?" Still no reply. More voices sound and I think I hear my brother Andrew now, but no. No. It's another voice. It's familiar. "Kane?"

I sway and someone catches me, someone big and strong. Unfamiliar. "Bitch is hot," the man says. "A good fuck."

"Stop," I say. "Stop. Let me—"

"Her fucking phone is ringing again"

My phone is ringing? Why can't I hear my phone ringing?

"It's Kane," another man says. Or no. Is it a woman?

I lose the moment. Everything is black. And then I'm in a car.

My eyes pop open as I remember something I'd forgotten until now. While everything was black, it wasn't completely black. There was a song in my head. My eyes go to the poster. That fucking song.

The sound of voices reaches my ears, the CSI team entering the apartment, and I shove down my emotions. I hate emotions. I hate that they want to settle in my chest and make me act like a fool. Inhaling a sharp as fuck breath, I reject them hard about five times before I win. Then, and only then, do I walk back into the bedroom and I stare down at Katy. She was drugged.

I was drugged.

We have a lot more in common than a Hollywood connection.

CHAPTER FOURTEEN

The CSI team comes in hard and fast, dispersing into the apartment, their presence forcing me to fight the adrenaline surging through me that tells me to go to the ring leader of the Society, Pocher himself, and kill him. Instead, I make my way to the front of the apartment, put on a jumpsuit, and stay right here on the scene, doing my job. I take photos. I look for anything that leads me to the person pretending to be a serial killer. It's not the first time I've thought that to be the case, but I'd dismissed that idea too easily. Because that's what this is. Someone pretending to be a killer to lead me on a chase, to ultimately kill me.

I believe this for the next hour until I don't anymore. I'm standing in Karen's completely clean kitchen, in a NYPD jumpsuit, staring at the sparkling sink, when I've finally calmed down enough to think straight. The fact that I have to calm down to think straight says that I'm not winning this matchup.

My cellphone rings, and I grab it to find Director Murphy calling. "Agent Love," he greets when I answer. "Why does everyone want you to go away?"

"Because I'm a pain in the ass," I say.

"Yes. You are. I understand you have a serial killer who likes you more than most of the police force."

"Are you worried about me, Director Murphy?"

"I do believe I'll bet on you over this Umbrella Man, as I hear you're calling him. Is there anything I need to know?"

Is there anything he needs to know? With Murphy, everything is coded. My job is ultimately about taking down the Society, which is why him supporting my involvement in this case makes me wonder if he knows there's a connection. Or not. I need to rein in my thoughts before I spew toxic waste that sounds like a crazy person said it.

"I see dead people," I say. "That's what you need to know right now."

"All right then," he replies. "You can tell me what you just decided not to tell me tomorrow. As for the dead bodies, make sure you're not one of them, so you can. Communicate, Agent Love. I feel I'll be reminding you of this the rest of our natural lives." He hangs up.

I shove my phone in my bag at my hip. Why didn't I tell him this could be about the Society? Because I think immediately if the Society were setting me up, why would they leave a clue for me to find that out? They wouldn't. That's the answer. They wouldn't. Bottom line, that night is still fucking with me. I let it find a way into my crime scene.

As for the song, maybe it's a coincidence, and I need to look for a different meaning. Maybe I didn't really hear it that night. I was drugged.

Like Katy.

Fuck.

I press my gloved hands to the sink again and lower my chin to my chest.

What am I missing?

"He's winning."

At Roger's voice, I cringe. I don't want to deal with him or his accurate statement right now. But I'll be damn if he and Umbrella Man get the best of me in one night. I push off the island and turn to face him. "Three dead women, one night. Yes. I'd say he's winning."

He gives me a heavy-lidded stare, it's a trademark "I'm judging you" stare. There's a reason I don't have a cat, or him, in my life right about now. Being judged ranks right up there with riding the subway next to a weird person who hasn't bathed in a year, who's picking bugs out of their hair and offering them to you for—who knows the fuck why they offer them to you.

I don't like to be judged. I need out of this kitchen.

"Let me help," he says. "We were good when we bounced ideas off each other."

He means when I craved his approval; a need I discovered once I left New York that actually shrunk my vision. I saw his way, never outside that box. Outside the box was where I needed to be and where I plan to stay. "I'd certainly like your analysis of the crime scenes tonight," I say because I won't turn down any resource that might lead me to Umbrella Man. I'll just use those resources my way. "We can talk tomorrow."

I walk past him, out of the kitchen, about to be out of his personal space that I want him to keep when he says, "If we team up, I do believe I can keep them from pulling you off the case."

There it is. His play at intimidation. I should have expected it. I turn and look at him. And I smile. That's all. I just smile. Not a happy smile. Not an amused smile. It's more an acid burn smile. I let it sit there, lingering between us, and then I walk away. I exit to the living room as Melanie walks in with Houston. Considering I know why Houston is here—to wet himself over the mayor while being a pain in my ass—I focus on Melanie. "Why are you here and not down in the rain, dealing with the bodies that could be affected by the elements?"

She puffs up, all indignant and proper, with her NYPD jumpsuit that's ten sizes too big with not a gun on her person. "I'm done with what has to be done. I wanted them moved out of those elements."

"Good," I say. "You can get to the lab and find out what poison he's using to kill them." It's with that statement that I realize my flawed reasoning a few minutes ago. I was drugged. These women were poisoned. That's not the same thing. It's a fact that has me mentally stepping back and rethinking where my mind has gone.

"Beth has the samples," she says. "We expect news on the toxin in the next forty-eight hours."

"Well, now you can get her another sample." I motion to the bedroom. "The victim was poisoned."

She purses her lips. "I'll go take a look." She walks away while I ponder the "toxin" that killed Umbrella Man's victims. I was drugged. They were poisoned. Two different things I turned into the same.

Houston steps in front of me, a linebacker in my path. "The elevator is fully functional," he says. "The crime scene is in basic procedural mode in the alleyway. I'm about to issue a basic statement about a suicide attempt, and one officer down in the efforts to save the victims."

Understanding is right there, in the air, where I could catch it and rub it in his face, but I stick with a simple, "Glad you and Director Murphy came to terms with my role here."

"I'll handle closing up the scene."

He needs control. I need out of here.

"But tomorrow—" he starts.

"We'll talk. We'll deal with all of this. Call me if there's anything significant that comes up during clean up. And have Sergeant Morris at the station tomorrow for official questioning."

"What the hell is that about?"

"Ask Morris. And I'll let you finish up the basics." I start walking, and I don't stop. I exit to the hallway, shed my suit in a disposal unit setup by the team, and I head for the elevator. I punch the button, and the car opens immediately, thank fuck.

I step inside the empty car, punch the button, and just stand there, watching the doors shut, a knot in my chest, a clawing sensation with it. The past is right here in this elevator. I reject it again and hard. I force myself to think about the investigation. That puts me back in the alleyway, hesitating because I don't want to get killed because of Kane.

Kane.

Fucking Kane.

I focus on him. That's a good thing. That's a bad thing. He distracted me. I thought about our engagement while investigating the murders. What the hell is this man doing to me? The elevator dings again, and I step off, a woman on a mission. Adrenaline burns through me and carries me to the door. I don't bother with the security codes. I ring the doorbell over and over, knowing that brings Kit to the door. I also know there are cameras, so when the bastard answers my door, in my apartment, and points a gun at me, that's all the invitation I need.

I draw mine and point it at him. "Leave."

"I'm not going anywhere," he spouts back.

"Except away," I say. "One way or the other."

"Take a dinner break," Kane says from behind him.

Kit grimaces with the statement that is all command, but he hesitates, his eyes burning angrily into mine before he lowers his weapon, shoves it in his holster under his jacket and then steps out into the hallway. Kane eyes my gun. "Planning to shoot me again?"

I holster my weapon. "I'll just use my fists."

He clearly doesn't think I'm serious because his lips quirk, amusement in his eyes before he backs up to let me enter the apartment.

I follow, ready for a fight.

CHAPTER FIFTEEN

I step inside the foyer, right in front of Kane, shut the door, lock it, and turn back on the security system. That I put that above a much-desired confrontation with Kane says I'm on edge. Umbrella Man is in the building. He may still be in the building, despite an automatic search that took place when the building was locked down.

I turn, and Kane is no longer standing in front of me. He's at the second door we must pass through to enter the apartment, the one that offers an extra level of security. He wants that extra level of security before whatever is about to go down between us, goes down. I know this, not just by his position at that door, but because Kane is now wearing his suit jacket again. That means he's ready to do business. For him, that means he's about to blow some shit up, perhaps not literally, but perhaps, quite literally. He's on edge, just like me, ready for anything.

I want him to blow up something, too, or someone: Umbrella Man.

I close the space between me and him and keep walking, exiting the door into the living room, letting him shut it and secure the entry, comforted by the fact that this place is like Fort Knox. Any attempt to get to Kane won't be while he's in this apartment. I'm suddenly back in that closet, staring at that poster with the U2 lyrics, and I start walking toward the kitchen. That takes me back to that parking lot in the Hamptons where I'd been kidnapped. What an idiot I was to even let that happen to myself and how was I drugged and Alexandra was not? And why am I thinking about this when three women died tonight? I'm not dead. I survived my shit, and they did not. They deserve my attention.

I enter the kitchen and walk to one of several bars in the apartment, this one is in a small enclosed area where he keeps the most expensive of his whiskey. There's no reason to lock it up because no one can get in here. Nope. They can't. Yet, Kane had a guard stay here with me when he was out of town, and he just had one with him. Whatever the fuck that means.

I grab the black bottle he told me cost him twenty grand. Fuck his twenty grand when he probably made part of it doing bad things. I'm living with a man who does bad things. And so do I, so I can't even judge him. God, I love that he does bad things. God no. No, I *do not* love that he does bad things. I just love the way he makes it seem so damn sexy. God no. He does not. Bad things are not sexy. I'm a fucking FBI agent. I'm also so very fucked up. I open the cap, slugging a swallow. It bites, but it's smooth in an instant. It shouldn't fucking bite at all for twenty thousand dollars.

Mr. Bad Things himself steps behind me.

I turn, and we both lean on the counters behind us, small counters, close together. His legs almost touch mine. I hate him for making me wish they were, at least right now. Sometimes, I don't hate him for making me want him at all. Now, I do, and he knows it. I see it in the slight narrowing of his eyes. He knows me. He knows me like no other person knows me, and he reads that funky place I'm in now. He thinks he knows how to handle it, too. He even took off his jacket and tie, like this war with me is no real war. He's right, really. It's not a war. Not between me and him. Not anymore.

It's a war within myself.

A war I'm not sure we can win, and some part of me is damn glad he's certain we can. Because I'm not.

I lift the stinking expensive ass bottle, toast him, and take another swig, daring him to tell me to stop. His lips curve and he reaches for it, taking it from me—because I let him, of course—and he slugs back a drink. Another thing I love about Kane—he can get ghetto when he needs to. Which also means he does bad things. Damn him for making me okay with bad things. And distracting me. I take another slug, the heaviness of the whiskey officially giving my head a little twirl, at least that's what it feels like. That and I'm pissed.

I set the bottle down. "You," I say.

"What about me, beautiful?"

"Don't call me that."

"What about me, beautiful?"

I growl. "Kane."

"Lilah," he says in that richly accented voice of his, that he chooses to make richly accented when he speaks my name. Because he knows I like it. Because back before I ever had my guard up with Kane, I told him I liked it. My guard isn't up with Kane anymore. It also wasn't fully up in that alleyway when it should have been because of Kane.

I step to him and grab his shirt. "Do you know what I did out there tonight?" I don't give him time to reply. "I hesitated because I didn't want to die. I didn't want to die because of you, Kane fucking Mendez."

He catches my wrists, both of them, and pulls me hard against him. "When did you ever not want to live, Lilah?"

"I'm talking about now, asshole. Tonight. I hesitated. I could have died."

He turns me and pins me in the corner, where the wall overreaches the counter. I don't let anyone cage me in, but Kane is Kane. And here I am. "I should have never left you alone for so long."

"I don't need a babysitter," I say. "And alone wasn't my problem. You are. You made me hesitate. I didn't want to die tonight. We're talking about tonight."

"You're supposed to want to live, Lilah. I let you feel the wrong things."

"You don't *let me* do anything," I say, punching at his chest. "You aren't hearing me."

He cups the back of my head. "You're supposed to want to live. And you're supposed to want to live life with me. We were engaged, woman."

"That was a long time ago."

"And here we are again. Back where we always belonged."

"With a serial killer stalking you and me?"

"There's always going to be someone coming after both of us," he says. "And if you think you're better off with no reason to live, you love me a whole lot less than I love you."

"That's not fucking true." I shove at him and force him to look at me. "I love you, but—"

His fingers tangle roughly in my hair, and he yanks my gaze to his. "Do not finish that sentence. Not now. Not ever. There is no but when it comes to us. And I'm going to kiss you right now, because you're mine, Lilah Love. You do not belong to the fucking Umbrella Man. He does not get to own you. Understand?"

"He doesn't fucking own me."

"Prove it."

"By letting you own me?"

"By doing what you always do and trying to prove I don't." He kisses me, and I start out doing just what he dared me to do. I kiss him back with one intention, proving he doesn't own me. Proving I own me. I alone fucking own me. I yank at his shirt and slide my hands under it, all the warm heat of his body stealing the chill of the rain and death that has haunted me this night. Things that don't always bother me, but they do tonight. He's right. Umbrella Man owned me tonight. It makes me angry, so damn angry, and I take it out on Kane. I shove against him, and he lets me. He backs up.

"Un-fucking-dress," I order.

His eyes darken as he pulls his shirt over his head and tosses it. This man shirtless is a distraction I need. I yank my bag over my head, right along with my badge. My shirt comes next, tossed aside, and by the time my bra is off, I'm against him. I'm kissing him, or he's kissing me. Whatever. He's doing what I want. He scoops me up, and he carries me to the living room—he clearly knows I'm in his bed, he doesn't need to force me there now.

He sets me down in front of the couch, and we're undressed faster than I was down that alleyway because I fucking hesitated. I shove him to the couch and start to climb on top of him. When I'm there, in control, his gaze rakes over my body, and his eyes meet mine. His lips curve, and I know I'm doing just what he wants me to do. He didn't want to own me. He wanted me to own me again. That's the thing about Kane Mendez. He knows I can't live in his world if I'm weak. I know I can't live in my world if I'm weak. But I also know he can't live in his world weak either. Suddenly, I don't care about who owns who. I just want to know he's alive.

I kiss him, and it's no longer a power play. I kiss the hell out of him and then whisper, "I need a break."

He understands. He always understands. He rolls us, and we're side by side, him inside me, him stroking hair from my face. "I'm here," he says. "You're here. We're just us right now."

"Yes," I whisper, and for the next, I don't know how long, that's all there is. Me and him. Him and me. But when we come back to reality, I'm back in that alleyway hesitating, and I know why it scared me so freaking badly.

"What happens when you hesitate Kane?"

"I'm not going anywhere."

"You can't afford to hesitate. You are Kane Mendez, and that's a dangerous name."

"The difference between us is that when you were gone, I never intended to let you stay away. I hesitated, I still do, because of you."

"You can't afford to do that." I try to get up, and he rolls me to my back, leaning over me. "A willingness to die is not power. It's not control. It's a source of stupidity."

"I disagree."

"Do you now?" he challenges. "You think a willingness to die helps you? You die, and Umbrella Man lives. Then he keeps killing. Seems like all he has to do is make you do something stupid to win."

He's right. "Damn you."

"Damn *him,* Lilah. Stop fearing the hesitation. Let it make you stronger. Let it make you smarter. Let it lead to the death of Umbrella Man."

The idea that there is more to this story, that Umbrella Man might know about that night, about my rape, starts to fester. And I'm good when I'm angry. The idea that he wants to come at Kane, that he is and has, provokes even more anger. "He wants to be the death of you," I remind him.

"And?" he prods, because he's good at prodding, at knowing when I've only given him half of what's in my head.

"And," I say, "I'm going to use that against him."

CHAPTER SIXTEEN

I'd throw my damn wet and bloody clothes in the trash, but they represent tonight's memories, and I need every trigger I can come up with that might help me kill or catch Umbrella Man. But I'm not putting them back on. I walk buck naked to the bedroom, right along with Kane, but I detour to grab my bag and badge. They belong in Purgatory. I belong in the shower.

Fifteen minutes later, we're both in T-shirts and sweats—yes, Kane Mendez and his arrogant self wears sweats—in the kitchen at the island. I'm filling a bowl with Rice Krispies because there's just something about the snap, crackle, and pop that does my heart good when I set the box down.

"Oh shit," I say, thinking of my bloody clothes again that I almost threw in a trash bag. "How is Jay?"

Kane grabs the box and continues to fill our bowls. "Good enough to tell me to tell you 'Fuck you, Lilah Love.'"

"Well, that's good," I say, pouring milk in our bowls, proving, once again, that anyone who says I can't work well with others is full of shit. The snap and crackle that follows is instant music to my ears and stomach, considering how hungry I am. "Kind of sad how scared he is of you," I say, sitting at the barstool next to me and taking a big bite of cereal.

"Anyone protecting you needs to be scared of me," he says dryly, claiming his stool, too, and digging into his cereal as well. "But they're usually scared of you."

I snort. "Whatever. It was you who freaked him the fuck out. He was a problem tonight. It affected when and how I dealt with that situation." I take another bite and wave my spoon at him. "Your ability to create fear in others might not always be your best foot forward."

"*You* never thought I was scary."

"I always knew you were scary, Kane." I soften my voice and mumble, "I just liked it a little too much."

"Enough to put a ring on your finger."

"That I took off," I counter, that night still there between us, and it's a barrier, it is, it has been for years, but it's shrinking.

"Because I buried a body for you. Some might think that's romantic."

God, I sort of do. "Most would not."

"And then there's you, Lilah Love." He hesitates and gives me one of his "I still have the ring" looks.

He still has the ring. I flashback to the crime scene and set my spoon down. "Are we really going there right now?"

"You know me well enough to know that I wouldn't go there over Rice Krispies. I'm just stating a fact."

My chest punches with the memory of taking off that ring and how damn much it hurt. Kane has always had a way of making me feel more human and less human than anyone else on the planet.

"I thought of that damn ring while in a dead woman's apartment tonight with her dead sister in her bed."

"He put this one on the bed, not the floor?" he asks, proving, as always, that the facts of my cases phase him not one little bit and that he goes where I go mentally with an ease I expect from no one else.

"Yes, and that's a message I haven't figured out, but we'll come back to that. The ring—"

"Yes, the ring. Tell me why you thought of it in that apartment."

I turn away from him and take a bite of my cereal, thinking about the question, thinking about the past. "That night," I glance over at him. "I was really happy you were coming home early. In the past, every time I think of that night, I think of all the bad, I think of the body and the knife and—that exchange we had before I was grabbed—that familiar wonderful way we were—"

"We're still those people."

I reject that idea. "I'm not the same person."

"You're better." He turns me to face him. "You *are* better, Lilah."

I turn to face him. "I found out I could kill and like it that night."

"No," he says. "That's not who you are."

"And what if it is?"

"You know what I think?"

"Why are you asking? We both know you're about to tell me."

"You use the moment you killed him to block out other parts of the night. It's easier for you to accept that part of you, to even vilify yourself in a broader way than it is for you to accept what he did to you. You're not that upset over who and what you are, Lilah. That person makes you damn good at your job. The monster you've made yourself is a way to hyperfocus on anything but the rest of that night. *That's* what I think."

He turns away from me and starts eating. I want to be angry or reject his words, but I can't. I don't even try. I'm not sure if they're right or wrong, but they don't feel wholly wrong, that's for sure. And so, I, too, turn away from him, and I start eating. I don't linger on his opinion, I can't. There are other words in my mind. The words on that poster, the song lyrics. That damn song *was* playing in the parking lot. And I didn't remember it until tonight because he's right. With all I've remembered about that night, there is still a lot I've blocked out.

"I hate when you're right," I say.

He glances over at me. "Because you hate to be wrong."

I give him a small smile. "I do hate to be wrong, don't I?"

He laughs, a low, deep rumble, before he says, "Understatement of the year."

I laugh, too, and this is one of those moments with Kane I missed so damn much. The moments when we find a way to laugh in the middle of hell burning around us. The laughter never lasts though. It can't last now. I shove aside my bowl, and I stop avoiding the past and where it took me tonight. Where it takes us. "He knows. Umbrella Man knows."

Kane shoves aside his bowl, and we rotate our stools to face each other, the massive apartment fading away. There is just me and him again. "He knows what?"

"About that night."

"He can't know about that night."

"And yet, he does, and he wanted me to know that he does. The victim who was in the apartment. She was naked, and he left her clothes in the closet in front of a U2 poster, with the lyrics for 'With or Without You' on it. I doubt it was organic to the apartment. He put it there. When I was grabbed, that song was playing on a radio somewhere in the parking lot or the car, I'm not sure which, I was too damn drugged."

He doesn't react. He just sits there, processing, and I know him. I let him. He needs to think. Seconds tick by, and he says, "He can't know."

"What other explanation is there?" I don't give him time to answer. "I thought about the Society setting all of this up to kill us both, but they wouldn't leave me a clue to figure out this is them."

"If you're right, and he was there—"

"I am. He knows."

"Then it's the Society," he concludes.

"He wouldn't warn me if it's the Society," I repeat. "But what if it's a rogue member or someone they hired to help that night? There were multiple people involved in my kidnapping."

"Or your first instinct was right," he says, "and the Society, not some rogue member, really is behind all of this. If they just kill me or you, for that matter, my people come after their people. If one of your cases appears to turn south on us, they avoid that."

"But they wouldn't leave a clue for me to figure it out," I repeat, more firmly this time.

"No one kills pigs and people who isn't really a killer," he says. "They hired someone capable of those things. Perhaps he sees you as a challenge. He left the clue because he's enjoying the game and because he thinks he's smarter than you. He feels like he can taunt you and still win."

"Maybe," I say. "That feels more right than wrong."

"It feels a lot right," he says. "The Society would also have access to Ghost and the money to pay him."

We share a look. "The Society," I say. "I knew we shut them down too easily."

"The Society doesn't want a war. That interferes in their bigger picture."

"Which is?" I ask.

"To quietly rule the world behind the scenes. Pocher's our problem. You take out Umbrella Man. I'll deal with Pocher."

He's right. They both need to go down, but something is bothering me. There's something in my mind, something I need to realize. "I need to go to Purgatory," I say, ready to seal myself in my thinking spot, the room off our bedroom. I push off the stool and start to walk away.

Kane catches my arm and looks up at me. "You aren't going to ask how I'm taking out Pocher?"

He's asking me if my badge is going to get in his way. "If Pocher's behind Umbrella Man, he's just as responsible for the murders as the killer himself."

"He's behind your father's political campaign."

"My father is a fool asking to end up dead. This isn't over. Someone else is going to die. I'd prefer it to be Pocher. I want it to be him."

And I guess that means I'm done hiding or turning myself into a monster.

Because I feel no guilt at wishing Pocher dead to a man who will make it happen nor do I mind one little bit that the man who will make it happen shares my bed.

CHAPTER SEVENTEEN

I'm on my headset, on the phone, calling Tic Tac by the time I make it to the bedroom. "I'd yell about the time," he answers, "but I heard you have three dead bodies tonight. Fuck. Yes, I said it. Fuck. What can I do?"

I pass through the bedroom and open the double doors to Purgatory, which is basically an office, but it's my office. It's my place to lock myself away until I catch this asshole. "What time is it?" I ask, entering the room.

"Here in LA, it's midnight, which means it's three there in New York City."

I'm not even sure how long it's been since this all went down. I sit down in one of the two chairs that decorate Purgatory. There's a desk and bookshelves, too, but the chair wins. "My 'I need' list is about to start," I say, "so take notes."

"Camera feed for every location you can get it. A history of everyone in the building who connects to the victims. I have the names. Murphy got them for me."

Murphy clearly had quite the talk with Houston. "You sound remarkably proud of yourself when Murphy told you what to do. I also need—"

"A profile for all victims. I'm on it all." Kane walks in, holding some sort of box, and sits down next to me. He opens the lid to display my favorite brownies. God, I really do love this man, like a fat kid loves cake.

I pick up a brownie and give him a pleased look. "Thank you."

"Did you just say 'thank you'?" Tic Tac asks incredulously.

"Yes," I say. "And don't say I don't say thank you. If you bring me brownies, I'll tell you thank you, too, unless they suck." I take a bite and make a fairly orgasmic sound before adding, "And these do not."

Kane smiles and winks, taking a bite of a brownie himself. I almost laugh because the truth is this man does scare the shit out of people, as proven by Jay tonight. And yet, right now, he's eating a brownie and looks like a little boy in a candy store doing it. "Kane brought you brownies?" Tic Tac asks.

I frown. "How do you know about Kane?" I demand, giving Kane a side eye and smiling.

'You told me about Kane, Lilah."

"He better know about me," Kane says. "Or I'll have to kill him."

"That's not funny," Tic Tac says. "Tell him I said that's not funny. No! No, don't tell him I said that. Ask him what I can do for him."

"Are you really that much of a suck-up, wuss?" I ask incredulously.

Clearly, Kane hears because he says, "Tell him I have my own people who I trust," Kane says, never looking over, half done with his brownie.

"He can trust me," Tic Tac argues. "Please tell him he can trust me. Director Murphy said—"

"What the hell?" I ask. "Murphy talked with you about Kane?" I glance at Kane who looks amused.

"He said Kane will help you, so we help Kane."

"Kane doesn't help you or Murphy."

"But he helps you."

"*You* need to freaking help me. I need a list of anyone involved in this that might have gone to a U2 concert. And, the year I relocated to LA, did they tour?"

"What does the year you relocated and U2 have to do with this?"

"Just find out." I disconnect, set my phone down and take a bite of the brownie. For several minutes, Kane and I sit there, lost in thoughts, each eating a full two brownies. Actually, I don't think much at all. The exhaustion of rain, blood, and murder is taking hold.

"Murphy really thinks he's hired you through me. Once you kill Pocher, I think I'll quit. After I kill Umbrella Man, of course. And this time, I'm not going to ask you to bury the body."

"You didn't ask me last time."

I pick up my badge from the table between us where I'd placed it earlier, and stare at it before looking at Kane. "I'm talking about killing people, Kane. What the hell is happening to me?" I set the badge back down on the table, *between us*, where he always says it exists. "I'm not even processing the damn case." I bury my hands in my hair and lean forward.

Kane goes down on a knee in front of me. I drop my hands and his settle on my knees. "You watched two people die tonight and dealt with a third in our own building. You faced down two killers: Umbrella Man and Ghost. You saved Jay's life. You visited the past. Of course you want the people who did this dead. You're human." He stands up and takes me with him. "It's three-thirty in the morning. I know how this works. You need to be at the station early. Let's sleep for a few hours."

"I should try to work the evidence."

"You will. *After* you sleep."

"You know if I didn't live with you—"

"You'd fall asleep on the floor," he says. "That's why Purgatory is right next to our bed." He leads me forward, and I don't fight him. He's right. I'm human. I'm exhausted. The heaviness in my body and the fog of whiskey, brownies, and too much adrenaline is winning.

A few minutes later, I'm in bed, in the darkness, Kane wrapped around me, like he's afraid I'm going to get away or do something really stupid like get killed. He doesn't say those things to me often, just as I rarely say them to him, but there are times, like now when I feel them when I know he feels them. We both know we're going to war—no—that we're *in* a war with the Society that never ended. I shut my eyes and try to force myself to sleep, but I swear I hear that damn U2 song in my head. Random parts come to me: *My hands are tied, My body bruised*. Words that don't fit my attack or the victims. But there's another line, one that feels like it's a message, four simple words that say so much: *I'll wait for you.*

CHAPTER EIGHTEEN

I wake to darkness, and the fact that my phone is silent has me sitting straight up. I grab it, reading the six am time. There are no missed calls. There are no text messages. My God, how are any of us sleeping after last night? Kane drags me back down to bed, wrapping himself around me, and orders, "Go back to sleep."

I lay there and will myself to do just that. I need to rest to think straight. I'm in a warm bed with Kane. Of course, I don't want to get up, but I have a bare minimum sleep of four hours that prevents further bloodshed at my hand, and my mind isn't going to let my eyes shut or my body rest. "We aren't going back to sleep, are we?" Kane murmurs roughly.

"You can, but I need to get up."

He presses his lips to my ear. "I'd give you a reason to stay in bed, but I don't like competing with other men. And I would be." He kisses my neck. "Catch the bastard so I can have you back." With that, he rolls out of bed and turns on the light. I roll to watch him pull on his pajama bottoms because, yes, I did just let a naked Kane Mendez get out of bed.

I turn away and climb out of bed myself, and yes, I'm naked, too, and no, I don't care. I'm primal if nothing else, comfortable in my own skin, not with what's beneath, but I'm working on that shit. I'm working on it hard. I just don't want to end up so damn comfortable that I'm like Michael Myers, walking around with a big ass knife in my hand. I like mine to stay in my boot.

A thought that transitions rather seamlessly to—I need to pee. I walk toward the bathroom. "You still have a great ass," he calls out, which makes me smile.

I don't look back though. Mother Nature calls more loudly than Kane Mendez, no matter how he might think otherwise.

A few minutes later, we both end up at the sink brushing our teeth. I have a moment that is surreal, and all about me and this man. It's short-lived as I think of three dead women who won't wake up and brush their teeth. I grab the counter and force myself to think of their faces, and I don't leave out Detective Williams. I'm not sure she's completely innocent in all of this, but she's dead. And she's innocent until proven guilty. My badge says so, even if I did leave it on the table last night.

Kane steps behind me and settles his hands on my waist. We share a look in the mirror that has nothing to do with sex or romance. I like that we compartmentalize these things. Rich was all about sex and love and smelling the flowers. I don't have time to smell the damn flowers, just Kane's neck here and there. And if he's lucky, I won't bite it, too. Kane gets that. He understands it, and so, this look is all about those murders and what comes next. It's ultimately about murder—and I like that it's about murder. We've hidden from too much in our relationship. I've hidden from too much period. I'm done with that shit.

"I'll make coffee," Kane says, releasing me and heading for the door.

He'll make coffee.

After having a silent conversation with me about murder.

For me, this is domestic bliss.

"Coffee is great!" I shout out, my version of "I love you," and instead of heading to Purgatory, where I want to be, diving into murder once again, I go to the shower. If I don't go there now, I won't get there at all. Bullshit is coming. That's how the morning after murder throws down, and I have to be ready to punch back when it punches me, and it will.

By the time I'm in jeans and a T-shirt at the bathroom sink, Kane is setting coffee in front of me. By the time he's out of the shower, I'm in Purgatory on the floor with a stack of notecards in front of me, intending to write out one for each person involved in the case, but first, I upload the photos I took last night. I tab through the shots, lingering on the one of Katy on the bed. I then find the prior victim who was on the floor and realization hits me. It's the ceiling fan. He placed the bodies directly under the ceiling fan. The location of the body wasn't the big clue I'd hoped it was.

I'm about to google lyrics to the U2 song when Kane walks in, dressed to kill in a gray pinstriped suit. And that's the thing, he's not just dressed to kill. There's an edge to him that says he's going to kill someone. The man who was eating brownies in this very room last night is not gone, just temporarily on a leave of absence.

Funny how, in the light of day, that feels like a problem; when last night, it did not, but now, I'm thinking about all the big players in this game, players as powerful as Kane.

"What are you going to do, Kane?"

He closes the space between us and squats down in front of me, his brown eyes almost black. "You don't ask those questions, Lilah. Don't start now."

"We talked about this Kane. We can't live together and be in that void. And I'm not trying to keep you from doing bad things. I'm trying to keep you from doing stupid things."

"I don't do stupid," he says. "Or you wouldn't be with me. You know what you need to know."

"I know what I need to know? Really? That's what you're going to say to me? We talked about this, Kane," I repeat tightly. "Secrets-"

"I have no secrets from you, Lilah. Just an understanding." He grabs the badge from the table. "And this." He takes my hand and presses it to my palm. "We made a deal last night. You do what you do, what this badge obligates you to do, and I'll do what I do."

"Pocher—"

"Is mine to deal with. That's our deal."

"Ghost—"

"Also *mine* to deal with."

"So that's where we're at, Kane? A deal actually means shut up and don't ask questions? Be careful how you answer. Me and my badge might get all sensitive and arrest you. Of course, we can fuck tonight if you make bail in time."

He stands up, and I do the same, ready for yet another war.

CHAPTER NINETEEN

Apparently, I'm the only one who wants a war because Kane does what Kane has done too many times in our relationship: he dodges and weaves. "Do you want a ride to the station?"

"Shut down like a side chick with red high heels."

"Lilah," he bites out.

"Kane," I bite right back.

"I'm protecting you."

"Stop."

"Never."

"Fuck you."

"Later," he says smoothly, too fucking smoothly.

"Fuck you again." My cellphone buzzes, and I glance at a text from Houston: *Shit is hitting so many fans it's raining shit here. The mayor is losing his shit, too. He has his own fan. The press is at his office. Where the hell are you?*

I glance at Kane. "I hate politicians, and my father is one of them."

"The mayor?"

"The moron? Yes." I shut my computer, and Kane and I both stand up. "Yes, to the ride. And as you go about your secret business—"

"Lilah—"

"Don't fucking 'Lilah' me in that arrogant, irritated Latin tone of yours. You're going to end up dead," I say, grabbing my field bag, packing my MacBook, and pulling it over my head and chest, "and then why the fuck did I move in with you?"

I head for the door, but I stop in front of him. "I thought after the other night, when you left on—" I lift two fingers and frame "'business' that we were beyond the secrets. I told you, Kane. I can deal with everything but that. Our deal was divide and conquer, not whatever the fuck this is you're

99

doing now." I don't wait for a reply. I give him my back and head for the door.

By the time I'm walking by the stairs, he's following me, like a freaking stalker, instead of the man by my side. And damn it to hell, I'm not in the mood for this. Kit is standing in the foyer, and I step in front of him. "Why are you here?"

"I'm your shadow today."

"I don't like you, Kit," I say, and when Kane joins us, I say, "Keep him with you."

"You like me, Lilah," Kit argues. "You were just cranky last night."

"I'm cranky every night. If you can't get along with cranky me, you can't get along with me."

"She has a point," Kane says.

My phone rings, and I glance down to find Houston calling. I answer the line. "I'm on my way now. I was actually going through evidence instead of talking about ways to hide it from the public." I hang up.

Kit immediately speaks. "I've been at this building for over a year. I can help. I see things. I know things that might help you."

"Sold. I don't hate you anymore but stay here. Work the building. Find out how the hell he got to her. Because he was in this building."

"I don't want you without backup today, Lilah," Kane says.

"I'm not a fool who turns down backup," I reply and turn to face him. "Unlike some people, I know when to face a dangerous adversary."

"You don't seem to know when to stop this morning, Lilah. With Kit present, would be that time."

"Jay almost died because he tried to be a hero. I'm not in danger. Not yet. And Kit does you no good. He's no match for Ghost."

"But I am."

"Because you're such a badass. Right?"

I step around him and head for the door. A few minutes later, we're in the back of an SUV with Kit behind the wheel. Kane and I don't speak. There's nothing I want to say in front of Kit. There's clearly nothing Kane is willing to say in front of Kit. If this asshole wants to assume he's the Latin King of the world and bulletproof, I can't stop him, and I have to live with that if I choose to live with him. But the secrets, those are a problem. They are going to that wall between us that won't come down.

We pull to the road where the station is located to find a horde of reporters. "Starbucks one block down," I order, long ago developing an escape and entry plan.

Kit does as I say and parks at the curb. I reach for the door, angrier with Kane right now than I realized. I need out of here before he finds out in a big way, right along with Kit. I exit the vehicle and Kane follows, shutting the door behind him.

I turn to face him, and he says, "I lined up another man to shadow you. He'll text you, so you can get to him if you need him. He won't do anything without your instruction."

I step to him, and I poke his chest. "Hesitation is bullshit. Don't fucking hesitate. That's not what this is about. Have the balls to tell me what you're going to do and believe I'll still be with you when you do. That's where I thought we were. Because you know what, as fucked up as it is, as fucked up as you make me, the only comfort I have is knowing that while Ghost is a killer, so are you. And we're the most fucked up couple on planet earth." With that, I turn and walk, not to the police station, but into Starbucks. Because I need a fucking white mocha before I deal with one more man today.

And yet, I walk to the counter, and a man offers to take my damn order.

Lord help him and Lord help Kane Mendez when I get him alone again.

And Lord help me because I'm an FBI agent who just wants him to kill everyone before they kill him. I manage to place my order, rather uneventfully, when my phone buzzes with a text that reads: *This is Zar. I'm Kane's man.*

I frown. Zar? His name is Zar? Someone's parents were doing too many of the Mendez drugs when they filled out the birth certificate. It's rather sickening though. Drugs. Kane's family is all about drugs. I've seen what drug overdoses do by way of dead bodies. I've arrested dealers, and I pretty much never think about Kane being a part of that world. Because he's not, I mentally push back. He's in oil, and he makes a hell of a lot of money in oil. The end. But he's the one I should be talking to about drugs that kill and are undetectable.

No.

He's not.

It's Beth, who is now in Europe, doing her medical examiner job there, instead of here, where she might end up a victim of the Umbrella Man. She also has special equipment and samples of the victims' blood, to get me my answers. I ignore the time in Europe and dial her now.

"Please tell me you got him," she says. "I heard there were more victims."

"We didn't. I need the toxin identified."

"Bad news on that. I ran the samples. I have nothing. I wish I was back there because there are things I'd look for now that I didn't, but I talked to Melanie. She's going down my list of suggestions."

"Fuck."

"Yeah ah fuck."

I crinkle my nose. "Stop saying that. It sounds weird when you say it."

"Coffee for Lola Love!"

"Jesus," I murmur. "Men are on my nerves today. Run the test again, Beth."

"I ran them three times."

"Try four. You're in Europe. You gained seven hours when you got there you can waste." I hang up and put my earbuds in before I grab my coffee. I need to call Kane with my hands free to drink coffee or shoot someone if they piss me off. I step outside, and I'm about to dial Kane when I think of Houston pretty much telling me Kane's under surveillance. I can't call him and ask him what I need to ask him while we're being listened to. Oh well, fuck it. I'm doing it anyway.

I dial Kane. "Did you call to apologize?"

"I don't apologize to assholes."

"Did you call to apologize?" he repeats.

"I need a drug that can be used to kill someone and not be detected on lab tests. If you don't know maybe that friend of yours who you have so under control does."

He's silent a beat, that turns into several, and I know why. I've assumed he's an expert on drugs. "I'll make some calls."

"Zar sent me a text. Who names their kid Zar?"

"Did you forget his name?"

"No."

"No one does."

I round the corner and grimace at the news trucks. "Oh, the joy of my job. I need to go." I hang up and cut right down an alleyway and then left. A few minutes later, my coffee is gone, I need to pee, and I'm walking in a side door of the precinct. I travel a hallway, pee, and then walk into the empty break area, which is the only way to get to the main department from this area. The TV is on, and there's a picture of my father speaking to a crowd, flashed by a newscaster saying, "The Love campaign is hitting the Governor hard and drawing big crowds." I stop walking and stare at the massive crowd being shown on the TV before the camera homes in on my father as he shouts, "I'm with you, never without you," and then U2's "With or Without You" starts playing.

CHAPTER TWENTY

My phone starts ringing, and I glance down to find Houston calling. I disconnect the line and press my hands to the basic table to my left. Aside from that being a weird as fuck campaign song, my father wasn't campaigning back when I was attacked. Did I hear that song in the parking lot or not? There's no in-between to this. It matters, and it matters because that poster on the apartment wall last night was a message. Either Umbrella Man told me that the Society is involved, which isn't the first time I thought he was giving me such a message. In which case, Kane could be right. The killer enjoys the game, and he doesn't think I'm good enough to figure out what he's telling me anyway. In which case, he's still a Society guy and so is my father, who is their golden child right now. That means my father is safe.

Or—

He's not with the Society. He's threatening my father, and I blew off the pig at his event as nothing more than a way for the killer to get attention and make the news. If this is all to cover up mine and Kane's murders, getting me in the news chasing this killer would feel like something they would want. But I can't be sure that's not the case.

His intended message comes back to my knowledge of that song.

And I never once remembered that song in connection to *that* night until *last night*. Now that I know my father knew about my attack, my mind could easily be connecting the song to him. If he's playing it on the campaign trail, I could have heard it before now. I probably *did* hear it before now, but considering my feelings about his run for office, I tuned it, at least partially, out. I squeeze my eyes shut and force myself back there again, back to that godforsaken night, back to the moment when someone grabbed me.

I sway and someone catches me, someone big and strong. Unfamiliar. "Bitch is hot," the man says. "A good fuck."

"Stop," I say. "Stop. Let me—"

"Her fucking phone is ringing again"

My phone is ringing? Why can't I hear my phone ringing?

"It's Kane," another man says. Or no. Is it a woman?

I lose the moment. Everything is black. And then I'm in a car.

I open my eyes. Everything was black. I was knocked out. There was no song. I've heard it played in relation to my father. That has to be it. That I turned it into a part of that night, because it's associated with him, says I have unresolved issues with him that I should probably solve with counseling. Or, by staying the fuck away from him. My shoulders relax. My father is not in danger. That I'm relieved after deciding to stay away from him might be illogical to some, but I don't have time for a funeral right now. This is all the Society, and they're involved with our family because of him.

I contemplate calling Kane, but this topic is dangerous, considering we're being listened to, so I text: *That problem you want to solve. It's the right problem to solve.*

He replies with: *You doubted that it was?*

My answer is: *Someone told me hesitation is good. I tried it. It doesn't work for me.*

He replies with: *What are you saying, Lilah?*

He thinks I mean we're a problem for me. I answer with: *I need to be more like you.*

For the moment, he agrees, which isn't his standard: *The badge keeps us in the middle routine.* It's an endorsement for "shoot first, ask questions later." Not that I need any shove in that direction, but my brother does. I dial him now. "I was about to call you. What the hell is going on over there? Houston says this serial killer is obsessed with you."

"We need to talk, but not on the phone, just make sure dad has extra security."

"Dad? He's locked down since the pig at his event."

"Just make sure locked down is really *locked down*. And be careful."

"What aren't you telling me?"

He doesn't get to hide in a dark corner and pretend he doesn't know what's going on anymore, but I can't talk about the Society on the phone. "This killer I'm dealing with taunts and kills family members."

"I know how to use a gun, Lilah. And the pig at the event made it pretty clear dad needed extra security. It's handled."

I open my mouth to tell him about the poster, but damn it, he's close to our dad. Dad is part of the Society. He might blab to dad and that's not a risk I can take. Not on the phone when I can't look into his eyes. "He likes poison, Andrew. Be careful. I need to go."

"What about that talk you just said we needed to have?"

"We're having it. Soon. Just not now."

"Lilah—"

I hang up, and I consider texting Kane again to make sure he has men protecting my family. But he does. I know he does. I trust him to look out for my best interests. I trust him more than my brother right now and that really sucks.

My phone buzzes with Houston again. I decline and head for the door when it opens, and Nick enters, his sleeves rolled up to show off his ink. Nick, the flirt and player, who'd been at the first crime scene and suggested I take an umbrella with me. "Lilah fucking Love."

"Nick," I say, and when my phone rings, this time, I don't bother to check caller ID. I know who it is, and I answer with, "I'm in the building. I've been trying to get to you."

"Where in the building?" Houston demands.

I hang up, and Nick walks to the coffee pot. "Heard you had a bad night last night," he says.

I start for the door but pause. "Were you on the scene?"

"I was off duty," he says. "Back on just in time to meet the press out front this morning. How many dead now?"

"Too many."

"Any leads?"

He and his hot boy attitude and curiosity feel off. In fact, he's bugging the fuck out of me. I turn to face him. "You were off duty last night. Maybe it was you."

He barks out laughter. "Tell that to Vivian. She's a hot blonde who works—"

"Get me her contact information."

He sets his cup down. "Are you serious?"

"As a lion hunting a deer," I say. "And you'd be the deer. Get me her contact information." I walk out the door, leaving him behind, with the sense that I'm in the warzone, right here, right now, in the police station.

Like maybe Umbrella Man is right here under my nose.

CHAPTER TWENTY-ONE

It takes me less than three minutes to get up the stairs and onto the floor where Houston waits and all but tackles me when I arrive. "My office," he orders.

Men.

Are.

Pissing me off today.

I follow him, proving that, every now and then, I can be obedient like that, though I doubt Kane would agree—but I do so now mostly because the little vein in Houston's eye isn't so little anymore. It might burst, and I do have medical training. A little. Not a lot. I can call an ambulance. He enters his office first, and I walk inside. He shuts the door.

"Other than trying to get me fired, what are we discussing?"

He scowls. "I was protecting you."

I laugh. "Such a pretty, nice boy you are."

Now he scowls. "The press got a hold of the truth. The words 'serial killer' are about to be all over the headlines."

"Okay," I say.

That vein throbs. "Okay?" he demands. "That's all you have to say, Agent Love? Because I was expecting more than 'O-fucking-K.'"

"First off, *Chief,* it's good to see you expanding your vocabulary. Secondly, he killed a pig and had it served at my father's political function. He wants attention. He probably told the press himself. Did we get anything on the pig farm by the way?"

"Yes. We got nothing. There were a shit ton of pigs. No one is going to notice or care about a few pigs that were swiped."

"You don't just swipe a couple of pigs. You fight them, wrestle them, and load them."

"And you know this from all your pig wrestling experience?"

"If you count a few men I've known, yes. And speaking of men, there was a pig in a dead man's bed. Did someone walk him up there like a dog? Have we walked that neighborhood and looked for someone who saw the pig get walked like a dog?"

"Pigs actually do get walked like dogs, Lilah."

"Not giant hairy pigs like that one, Mr. Someone Pissed in My Cheerios Today."

"You, Lilah. You did."

"And I take that as a no. No one went door to door asking about the pig. You didn't want to risk the bad press a dead pig in a bed gets you?"

"You're thinking about your case. I'm thinking about an entire city."

"Someone saw this."

"He wiped out the cameras surrounding your father's event," he snaps. "You think he can't handle some pig farmers or an apartment building?"

He's right. He could. He's right, and I no longer wonder how he has the resources to do such things either. He has the Society behind him. And the Society is close to my father. An idea hits me, and I pull out my phone and text Tic Tac: *I need a list of political contributors to my father's campaign.*

Houston's cellphone buzzes with a text that he glances at and then me. "Sergeant Morris is here. He wants to talk to you."

"I'm sure he does. Put him in an interrogation room. And I need to meet with the team."

"They're all upset over Williams. They can't handle your shit today."

"Oh Jesus, Houston. Aside from Williams making a shamble of the first crime scene, she set me up. She called me into that alleyway and into a booby trap. And yeah, I get it, I had more a shot at survival than her sorority sister—that we all should have fucking known about—but that's another topic. She didn't represent the badge, and I'm still not convinced there's not more to it than that."

"And you think you do?"

"Ah," I say. "I see. That's our problem, is it? You don't think I represent the badge."

He scrubs his jaw. "I didn't say that."

"You damn sure said enough. What's the problem, Houston? I get the job done differently than you, so I don't deserve my badge?"

"I'm not going down this rabbit hole with you, Agent Love. Not now. We have bigger things to deal with."

"Bigger than your balls, *Chief,* that's for damn sure. I'm going to leave before I try to find them and yank them out. Which could be embarrassing for us both since they're so fucking small." I reach for the door.

"Don't trash Williams," he warns. "I came here to clean up the department. I can't have a serial killer and a bad cop in the press at the same time. I'm sitting in on the meeting."

"Meetings," I correct. "I'm formally interviewing them as co-workers of Williams. And, are you sure you have time? Shouldn't you be changing the mayor's diaper?"

"He's just sitting on the shitter and staying there. He's avoiding the press today and told me to get him something 'good' to say tomorrow, or he'd find someone who could."

"The Pats are 6-0. Now you have something good to tell him. Take some time to do that because if you come into my meetings and overstep, we'll have problems." I exit his office and leave him there to try to grow those balls back. Unless that was all an act. Why the hell does it feel like it was an act but to what end?

I walk down the hallway and enter the empty office I used once before, sitting down behind the desk. I'd say he was too cowardly to be Umbrella Man, but he still got to the crime scene too fast, like he knew it was going to happen. That begs the question: is he with the Society, placed here to be their eyes and ears? My answer is maybe. Which is why he now gets only "need to know" information and not much of it. And why, as eager as I am to get back to Purgatory, more and more, it's feeling like all the answers I need are right here, in this building, which means I'll be staying awhile.

I stand up and exit the office just in time to watch Sergeant Morris walk into Detective Williams' office, and Roger is with him.

CHAPTER TWENTY-TWO

Roger wants to piss me off.

He's territorial. He clearly can't step back and let his protégé take the lead. One might say that I'm territorial as well, and I am. There are elements to this investigation that I'm not bringing to his attention. The old bastard will end up dead. He just doesn't get that.

And he clearly didn't spend much time getting to know me in those years we spent together, or he'd know, I don't react to these types of games. Not that I don't react well. I just don't react. I've known for a long time that I'm missing certain emotional chips. I hide that behind being hot-headed and loud-mouthed, by intent. It's calculated. And it's why I can sit across from a killer without unease. It's also why I'm not going to burst into the office and break up the interview. At this point, he's changed the tone of my interview with Morris.

It's done.

I'll take it in stride.

I walk past the door, and I've made it all of a few steps beyond it when I hear it open, almost as if someone called and told them I was passing. I don't turn. I keep moving, but Roger isn't letting that fly. "Lilah."

Not Agent Love.

Lilah.

I'm no fool. That usage is meant to remove my FBI badge from the hierarchy. Been there, dealt with that before, and will deal with it again. I clench my teeth and turn to face him and Morris. Morris who is in his uniform despite being suspended. "Anyone know where I can find the donuts?" I ask.

"I don't believe I've ever seen you eat a donut," Roger says, wearing dark-rimmed glasses today.

"I pretty much inhale them, so I could see you missing the twelve dozen I must have eaten while working for you."

I motion to the glasses. "Your eyes are bad now, huh? Does the cigarette smoke fog those up?"

"I stopped smoking. Well, some days, occasionally. And my eyes might be bad, but my mind is just fine."

Except he didn't know I love donuts or that I don't really get taunted all that easily. Umbrella Man he is not. I eye Morris, who is making a sour face. "Why do you look like you swallowed a bad egg whole. Without peeling it first?"

"I'm on leave. I didn't do anything wrong."

"I guess your answer is, 'I'm pissed off and that's the face I make.'"

"He's working under me," Roger says. "I'll take responsibility for him."

My gaze shifts to Roger, and I laugh. "He's your new protégé?"

"Why is that funny?" Morris demands.

Because Morris mocked my handling of the scene last night while behaving like an adolescent boy going through a pubescent testosterone rush, I think. I'd say that out loud, but he might have a meltdown, and I don't have a towel to offer him. "Inside joke," I say, and when he eyes Roger, I add, "With myself." Now I glance at Roger. "Were you questioning him or calming his frazzled nerves?"

"Seriously, Agent Love," Morris says, "do you have to be this much of a bitch?"

He took my bait, and I go in for the kill. "No. But it's easier for me if I am. Is being a 'little bitch' easier for you?"

Men really do hate being called a little bitch, and he scowls appropriately. I don't believe Umbrella Man would any more than I would. "I want Roger to interview me," he says.

"I want a triple chocolate cheesecake. We all want, but we don't always get what we want. Meet me in the interrogation room."

"What about my leave?" he asks.

"We'll talk," I reply, "in the interrogation room."

"Do as she says," Roger urges. "Go. Now."

He doesn't "go now" before he gives me another scowl and says, "I didn't hurt her."

"Sergeant Morris," Roger snaps, and then finally, Morris walks around me and leaves.

Roger steps closer. "He's a good man, Lilah."

"Okay."

Amusement, not anger, lights his eyes. "You're a piece of work, my girl. There's a reason I picked you."

"Like there's a reason you picked him?" I challenge.

"That's right. There's a reason. I'll leave now and let you do your job. I emailed you notes." He steps partially around me and pauses to softly say, "Poison's a female weapon, but you know that. I was your teacher." And with that, he leaves.

He's right, of course. Statistically speaking, yes, poison is a woman's weapon of choice, but I don't second guess myself because of Roger. Umbrella Man guts pigs. But I think about the reasons for using poison. He's smart, really damn smart. Who would know using poison made us think this was a woman? The answer is simple, and it takes me a place I've already considered. Umbrella Man is someone in law enforcement, someone in forensics. They'd know how to choose a poison and drown the evidence.

My mind goes to Beth and my reasons to get her out of the country. I suspect now that I did what he wanted. I got her out of that lab. Because she was close to him. Because she had eyes on him and didn't know it.

CHAPTER TWENTY-THREE

I'm still walking, headed to talk to my team, if you can call them that, when it hits me that I'm planning to talk to them about Williams. Because I considered Williams a suspect.

Fuck me.

Maybe he's not a man. Maybe Roger is right. I considered a woman while screaming that the killer is a man. It's not like I won't shoot someone, and I'm a woman. It's not like I couldn't make someone kill a pig for me. Actually, I could do it myself. I just wouldn't like it. Animals are innocent, pure, free of human bullshit. But I'd do it to save a life, while our killer might do it because taking a life is as sacred as saving one can be to me. Okay, taking a life can sometimes feel pretty sacred as well, but that's a whole level of fucked up I have that isn't normal.

I don't know if I should curse Roger or thank him for opening up my thinking. I've been known to be stubborn when I decide I know the killer, even if I haven't met that killer yet. I'm normally right, but I'm painfully human at my core, even if some, me included, could argue differently. In other words, I'm not always right.

I weave through the cubicles to find everyone on our team missing from their designated locations.

Rounding a corner, I enter the conference room, and there I find Houston along with Sally and Lily, two of our staffers, sitting in chairs forming a circle. Also present in that circle is the weird-ass freak of nature, Thomas Miller, the redheaded forensics guy, and my opinion has nothing to do with his looks. He's a decent looking thirty-something guy, who just happens to exude a creep factor level eight out of ten. Houston, literally, had to have rushed down here in the three minutes I was in the empty office. He's babysitting me alright. But is he protecting himself or the Society?

Or both?

"There she is," he states, as Lily, the twenty-something teenager of the group, based on her display of maturity, swipes at her eyes.

"I can't believe she's dead." She sobs.

I'm demonstrating that missing emotional chip, I know, but I hate tears. Like, I really, really hate tears, especially those shed at the office. What purpose do they solve besides making a woman look weak and a man look like a bitch ass loser? Thoughts I'm allowed because they didn't leave my mouth. But they might. I really can't make myself any promises right now.

"She had a sorority sister she treated like family," I say. "Why didn't we know?"

Lily bristles. "She never told us she had a sorority sister she was that close to."

I don't even bother to step inside the doorway. "We don't research a case based on what we personally know. We research based on facts. If this team is too personally involved to do a proper job, we need to adjust the members."

"I'm not emotionally involved," Sally says, her wild brown curls straightened today, her fifty-something skin newly glowing, her eyes crystal clear. She's not been crying. She's been to the damn spa. How very cold and removed she is. "I knew her work persona," she adds. "That's all. That keeps this clean for me. What do I need to do?"

"Your job," I say. "What is it?"

She doesn't bristle. At all. I think about our last encounter. She wasn't this removed. "I've started fact-checking witnesses' stories," she says. "Including those who live in the building where Karen lived."

"I loved her," Thomas interjects.

My gaze jerks to his. "You loved Detective Williams?"

"Karen," he amends. "I recorded her show every day. I watched it at night."

"You watch a soap opera every night," I say. "How very *different* that is."

He bristles. "Do you know how many men watch that show?"

I have three bristlers, including Houston, and one cold as ice bitch. Two, if you count me.

I eye Sally. "Get me those stats on how many men watched her show and find out if she had any stalkers. It's a weak prospect for a suspect since she wasn't the first victim, but we need to rule it out."

"No reports of stalkers for any of the other victims," she replies. "And I already looked that up for Karen as well being that she was an actress. It felt logical. No formal reports."

She's efficient. Thank fuck for her. "Do we have any word on DNA on scene?" I ask.

"I'm working with the forensics lead who was at the scene last night," Thomas says, sitting up straighter. "But from what he's given me thus far, there's not much to work with. Rain's a real bitch."

"Email me the data they collected," I say, pulling my cards from my bag and tossing a stack on the table. "In case anyone needs to reach me, I'll be in the building, but text me, call me, email me when appropriate." I eye Thomas again. "I need a list of everyone who is working forensics on this case and the connected cases. Now."

He nods.

"This is where you stand up and go do it."

"Oh right." He stands up. "I'm going to do it."

He leaves the room, and I eye Lily. "We had a dead pig in an apartment. Go door to door and tell them you're from the Humane Society, and you have reports of a pig on the premises. Find out if anyone saw the pig."

"She can't go alone," Houston says.

"I can't go alone," Lily agrees, pushing to her feet. "I'm scared."

I eye Houston. "Do you have an officer who can do this in plain clothes?"

"I'll handle it," he says, but I wonder if he really will. I also feel like Lily's fear doesn't match her job.

I walk into the room, shut the door and sit down in front of her. "What aren't you telling me, Lily?"

She bursts into tears. "I didn't know," she says. "I didn't know."

My eyes meet Houston's shocked stare before they return to hers. "You didn't know what?"

"She hated me. She hated me for a good reason, but I didn't know."

"What reason, Lily?"

"I went out with Sergeant Morris. It's allowed. He's not my supervisor. I met him here at the office. I didn't know he was here because of her. She was in love with him, but she was seeing Ralph Redman." Her voice lifts. "She was with Redman. I didn't know. And the last thing she said to me was that I was dead to her."

Fuck.

Here is a woman I feared was close enough to Williams to become a victim. Now, I'm worried she was close enough to Morris to become a victim.

I motion to Houston, and he nods. "Stay right here, Lily," I order, and she sobs, giving a choppy nod.

Houston and I move to the door, step outside and into an office, where he shuts the door. "I didn't know," he says.

But he should have. "*You're* dead to me," I say. "How do you not know this?"

"Detective William's is dead. She can't hurt Lily."

But Morris could, I think. Thankfully Kane has someone watching her but from who?

A man. A woman. What if Umbrella Man is both? What if it's a group of people? The man thought to be the Son of Sam claimed it was a cult doing the killing. Isn't that exactly what the Society is? A cult? "Too many people connected to Williams are now dead." I reach for the door and meet his stare. "If she ends up dead, I blame you. And I don't ever leave my blame unanswered." With that, I open the door, and right when I'm about to exit, I hesitate. What if she was crying because she's more involved than she's letting on? I turn back. "Find out where she was last night." With that, I exit the office.

I'm going to chat with Sergeant Morris. He knows something he's not telling me, but he will. He will today, this very day, or lord help me, he'll be the one crying.

CHAPTER TWENTY-FOUR

The elevator breeds conversation and my irritation like a cheater breeds STDs: in painful excess. Since I'm saving all my mammoth irritation for Sergeant Morris, I take the stairs.

The walk is two floors, and it's not long until I enter an area where a woman in uniform sits between me and the interrogation rooms. Not sure when this kind of security became necessary, but whatever. I don't know her. That's what matters. No need to converse. I flash my badge. "Where's Morris?" I ask.

"3E," the woman in uniform states, motioning me down a hall.

I walk in that direction and ignore the detective who passes me, despite vaguely remembering him from the past. I'm focused. I'm on a mission, and it isn't to the damn moon, though it might be to hell for Morris. I enter a room where an officer is running the recording equipment; I give him instructions before I enter the room where Morris waits. He stands up. I slam the door. "Sit down," I order.

He doesn't.

Of course. He's a man. You have to bust his balls to get him to listen to a woman, which is fine. I'm good at busting balls.

I walk to the table right across from him, shove my hands on the top, and lean toward him. "Lily told me you fucked her."

He pales.

"Sit the fuck down," I say.

He sits.

That was the easiest ball-busting ever.

I sit, too. "Start talking," I order.

"Why is this an issue?"

"Why did you turn pale as a ghost when I said I knew then?"

"Because you came into an interrogation room and threw that out like you meant for it to cut me."

"Apparently, it cut Lori. She was pissed at Lily."

"That doesn't even make sense. We broke up. She was dating someone else. We were *just* friends at the time. I told you we weren't compatible as a couple."

"But you were friends."

"We were better as friends than we were at dating. I could laugh at her being a slob as a friend. When you date someone, you think—could I live with them? And why keep dating if the answer's no?"

"How did you meet?" I ask.

"A charity run two years ago."

"Lily says she met you when you were here to see Lori."

"Technically we 'met' when I was dating Lori, but we never really spoke until that charity event. Why is this important?"

"You could have dated Lily to stay close to Lori, Detective Williams."

"I was already close to Lori. We still hung out."

"Did you know her new boyfriend, Redman? You know, the one who shot himself in court to try to save her life."

His lips tighten. "I knew him. I hung out with him and Lori a few times. I didn't like the guy. And he didn't seem like he was into her enough to shoot himself to save her, but you know, what do I know?"

"Explain," I order.

"He took a few calls that felt off. Secretive. Like side chick kind of calls."

"Sounds like you have experience with side chicks."

He scowls. "A guy who's been around other guys with side chicks knows shit, too."

Maybe, I think, but there's another possibility. Redman was texting the Society, and I wonder if Redman was actually the one who pulled Detective William into the Society but somehow crossed them himself. I pull my phone out of my bag and text Tic Tac: *Look for any connections of the victims or members of law enforcement associated with my current cases to our friends. If you don't know what that means, ask Murphy.*

He replies instantly: *I know stuff, Lilah. And I've already been working on that task.*

I'll have a few remarks to make about his "know stuff" declaration later.

"I didn't do this," Morris says, dragging my attention back to him.

I shove my phone back in my bag. "Give me something to make me believe you."

"The time of death. I was on duty yesterday, and I wasn't alone. I couldn't have killed those women."

"And yet that scratch on your face means nothing."

"I told you—"

"DNA will show up under fingernails. You know that, right?"

"Yes." He flattens his hands on the table and leans toward me. "I wasn't alone when I got this. Ask Travis Burrows. He was with me. He's a well-respected veteran of the department, as am I. I've been here fifteen years."

"I've known a lot of dirty cops that were," I frame my next words with my fingers, 'well respected,' as you say." I lean back and study him. "Were either of you wearing a body camera?"

His lips thin. "No. The department is battling a shortage of gear."

I change topics. "Did you tell Roger about Lily?"

"No. Why would I? We went on a few dates. That's all. And yes, Agent, we fucked. I did not, however, fuck Williams. The friend thing. We figured that out before we made the mistake of getting naked together."

"So, you and Lily aren't still dating or fucking?"

"No."

"You go on a few dates with a lot of women?"

"Last I heard," he snaps, "that's not your business."

"Only if you kill them."

He leans forward and slaps the table. "I didn't fucking kill anyone. I serve this badge." He points at said badge. "I do my job and beyond, every single day of my damn life. I risk my life to serve and protect. I loved Lori. She was my friend. She was one of us. This is my place in the world, and you take it from me, for doing nothing but caring?"

He's got about five too many emotional chips, five too many to be our killer. Just the right amount to be blackmailed. "Did anyone ask you to do anything to save Detective Williams?"

"No, I was not blackmailed," he says. "I'm not stupid enough to believe if I kill myself like Redman supposedly did, that she gets to live. And yes, I know the details of the case. I asked around."

He means Roger told him.

Fucking Roger.

"What did you talk about with Roger?" I ask.

"My suspension."

"And he said?"

His lips thin. "To tell you the truth."

He cuts his stare, lying as he declares he was told to tell the truth. Roger said something else to him. Whatever the case, I'm done with him and Roger. I stand up and walk to the door, glancing over my shoulder, to say, "Go back to work." I don't wait for his reply. I exit the room and find Houston waving to me from another room.

Houston, who is just a little too in my face right now.

I consider walking on past him but who knows what desperation—his new nickname—might do if left unsupervised. I close the space between me and him and step inside the room with him, aware that this could be filmed, and I don't like it. "Well?" he asks.

"What didn't you see on camera that you want to know, Houston?"

"Your opinion."

"I sent him back to work," I say. "That should say it all."

"I don't like the Lily thing," he says.

"Have Morris watched. If he's lying, you'll know."

"Who the hell is going to watch him? Everyone likes him. They'll protect him. Can the Feds handle this?"

"Can I handle it? Yes."

My cellphone rings, and it's Beth's number. I answer. "I know what it is. I know what the poison is. I ran a test on a whim. I read about a case and—"

"Hold that thought," I say, glancing at Houston. "I'll call you right back." I disconnect and talk to Houston. "I'll handle Morris. Get someone out to ask questions about the pig. I'll talk to Sally later today. Anything else?"

"The mayor. The press. The serial killer story is out there."

"Do the obvious. The killings are not random. The general public is not at risk. The end."

"We don't know how he or she picks their victims."

He or she. Roger has been running his mouth. "Yes, we do. This is personal, this is about me, which is why you tried to get me fired."

"I tried to protect you."

"What you fail to understand, but Murphy does, is that when someone tries to bend me over, I get all excited about the moment they learn that it's me who is going to bend them over. Tell that to whoever needs to hear it." I turn and head for the door.

"What the hell does that even mean, Lilah?"

"You can figure it out," I say, glancing over my shoulder at him. "I have confidence in you."

I exit the hallway and start walking, grabbing my phone as I do to redial Beth. "Tell me," I order.

"I was reading an article about a teen who poisoned her father. The only way we found out in law enforcement was she told a friend."

I enter the stairwell and stop walking, out of fear the service will cut out. "How does that help us?"

"I tested for that drug that that teen used, and it came back positive, Lilah."

"Holy hell you're good. What is it?"

"Barium acetate. It's used for a variety of commercial reasons like drying paints and varnishes, but in chemistry, it's a tool to prepare other acetates. It's a catalyst in organic synthesis. Bottom line, it's lethal if ingested, and we don't commonly test for it."

"Where would one get it?"

"It could be in a manufacturing facility for paint, lubricants and a variety of other things. Or in a lab—this teen, who killed her father, got it from her high school science lab."

"Do you have it in your lab here?"

"I've ordered it on a few occasions, but the forensics teams are more likely to have it on hand."

"Are you sure you don't have any in stock?"

"I don't know. I don't think so. What are you thinking?"

That I was right. Someone in forensics or even the medical examiner's office is involved in this. It's not the first time I've thought someone might have wanted Beth out of the picture. And when Beth left, Melanie took over the case. "That you're a badass chick who needs to keep your ass in Europe until further notice." I disconnect.

It's time for me to visit the medical examiner's office.

CHAPTER TWENTY-FIVE

I text Zar on my way down the stairs: *Leaving through the same door I came in. If you don't know where that is, meet me at the medical examiner's office.*

North or South, he replies back.

I don't do North or South, I answer. *The door closest to Starbucks.*

His response is fast: *There are four Starbucks within a mile radius, which I know because I drink a lot of Starbucks.*

Zar loves Starbucks. Who'd have thunk it?

I type: *The one that's really tiny and has some sort of statue out front.*

Okay, he replies.

Okay.

That's what I'd said to Houston that had really pissed him off, but really, what's wrong with that answer? It's an acknowledgment, minus messy emotion. Much like Roger saying yes. He chose Morris for a reason. He didn't get defensive. He didn't explain his reasons either, but I didn't expect that he would. A lot of people would feel the need to explain, though. And what is this thought process telling me? God, I need to get to Purgatory because I can feel myself trying to realize something. I need calm, quiet, alone time.

I finish my walk and exit to the breakroom again, only to stop dead in my tracks when I find Roger and Lily sitting at the table playing that fucking game of cards. All of them, all the damn card games. He used to make me play them, too. "New trainee?" I ask.

Lily is sitting with her back to me and twists around. "Oh God no. He's just helping me use my lunch hour to calm my mind and think about the investigation."

Roger's lips twitch. "Worked for you."

It never fucking worked for me. I just wanted to beat him, and then when I figured out how, he was pissy about it.

So, I started pretending to lose. "I thought you were leaving," I say.

"I was grabbing a cup of coffee for the road and then Lily burst into the break area crying. And, here we are."

He hates crying more than I do, as in, it all but makes the man twitch. And yet he stayed? What the fuck am I missing? What does he know about Lily and Sergeant Morris that I don't because that has to be what this is? He thinks there's a connection between her and the murders. I don't. And if he's right and I'm wrong, he'll tell me while gloating later. I can handle that. I head for the door. I expect to have to repel Roger. I don't. He lets me go.

Good.

If he's that into her as a suspect, I can focus elsewhere.

I head toward the subway and dial Tic Tac. "Yes, your highness."

"This guy you're dating is making you quite the smartass."

"Why would you blame him?"

"Whatever is new shines the brightest until it burns out."

"And if it doesn't burn out, then what?"

"Rare," I say. "But it happens." I don't wait for an answer. "I need to find out if any lab in the city ordered barium acetate or if anyone connected to the case has access to it."

"Is that the poison used?"

"Yes. That's it. Apparently, it's common in labs, and it may be hard to pin down, but I need you to do it anyway."

"Right. It's hard. Tic Tac to the rescue. Changing topics: Political donations to your father's campaign. A long list of law enforcement. He's their guy. They love him."

And my father apparently loves the Society, who if I'm correct, just killed those three women last night. Who I'm certain is behind my mother's murder. "Anyone I need to know about?"

"It's everyone. They did some event for him. Just about everyone in the building donated at least five dollars a week from their paychecks, including Detective Williams. Larger donations came from your old mentor, Roger. That new

Chief, Chief Houston, but they donated the same day as the drive. And they make a lot more money than the rest."

"In other words, this is getting me nowhere."

"Not necessarily. Redman and that soap opera star also donated. Her sister did not, but she lived in California."

Which might confirm my idea that Redman was the Society. But knowing Williams' sorority sister donated makes me wonder if she was, too, and with Williams the common denominator, was she the one who got them involved? Maybe that's why she called me into the alleyway. She was helping the killer and didn't expect to die. Ghost had a different plan. I can't prove any of this, but that's where Tic Tac comes into play.

"What about those connections to Pocher I asked about?"

"Chief Houston and Roger were at the same fundraiser for your father you were at, as were hundreds in law enforcement. I'm still working."

"Look at Redman's caseload. Look for someone with ties to the Society who he might have represented." I'm about to be at the tunnel. "I'm going on the subway. I'll be back online in a few minutes." I hang up, and that's when I feel someone at my back.

CHAPTER TWENTY-SIX

I walk another foot, weave into the crowd and then step into an alleyway. Someone follows, and I easily grab that someone. The woman yelps and I shove her against the wall. "Agent Love," she rushes to say. "Agent Love, it's me. Sally."

I blink her into view and scowl. "What the hell, Sally? Why are you following me?"

"I wasn't. Or, I was, but not like *following you*. Just trying to catch up. I was going to Starbucks and I saw you."

And yet, when I weaved into the crowd, she managed to keep up. That doesn't read like an average person "catching up," but then I'm a paranoid bitch right now. "Why didn't you just shout my name or call my phone?"

"I called out. I did, but there were sirens."

"I didn't hear a siren or you calling me. Why are you here with me right now, Sally?"

"I needed to tell you something I didn't feel comfortable saying at work. I was going to call but not while I was at work."

She's stating facts. She's not emotional, thank fuck. I release her and fold my arms in front of me. "Talk."

"Thomas was really obsessed with that soap opera star. He found out that Detective Williams knew her, and he was all but stalking Williams to get her to introduce him."

It's a red flag I should have seen and probably would have if I could ever get to Purgatory. "How do you know this?" I ask.

"Aside from witnessing it, Detective Williams complained about him. I know there were more murders that don't connect to Detective Williams, but maybe they connect to him. I've tried to investigate, but my resources aren't broad enough. And I'm not a nervous person, *at all*, but he creeps me out."

My hands go to my hips. "How close were you to Williams?" I ask, and yes, I know I asked this earlier. People change their answers like a woman changes her hair: every time they suddenly want to show the world a new side of themselves, and often, it seems, just fucking because.

"I told you," she says. "We had a professional relationship. No outside work contact."

"Do you have a relationship with Sergeant Morris?" I ask.

She shakes her head. "No. I met him once. That's all."

"Did Detective Williams talk about him?"

"Yes. She really liked him."

"I thought you didn't know her beyond work?" I challenge.

"We've worked, or worked," she amends with a swallow, "we worked together for years. I could read her, and when she talked about him, she softened."

"And Redman? Was she into Redman?"

"I don't know," she says. "But she didn't talk about him. She still talked about Sergeant Morris."

She still talked about Morris, I think.

He's the one who could influence her. He's admitted a need to be obsessively clean, which fits our killer except that feels more staged to me than anything. And the killer doesn't suck his thumb every time something goes wrong. Morris does, and unless he's a damn good actor, he's not him. And the idea that he is that good of an actor, well, that's a tough sell. Me being a bitch to hide my lack of emotions is a far cry from him acting like the little bitch I called him to cover up being a psychopath.

But it's not impossible.

"Agent Love?"

I snap Sally back into view. "Go back to work or to Starbucks or wherever the hell you were going." I leave her there, round the corner and start walking, thinking about Thomas. He's in forensics. He's creepy. He openly admitted to having a crush on one of the victims, but Morris just keeps grabbing my attention. Thomas feels too obvious. Maybe Morris really is a perfect faker. I dial Tic Tac again.

"That was a fast ride."

"There's a Sergeant Morris who I need you to look into."

"Yes, he's on the list of law enforcement on the scene last night," he says.

"Does he have access to the toxin I have you researching?"

"Are you fucking serious, Lilah? I've had about five minutes to work on this."

"Language, Tic Tac. *Language*."

"Sorry. Sorry, you just—you—has anyone ever told you you're overwhelming."

"No, but you're a wuss. Does he have access to the drug, Tic Tac?"

"The division of labs out of Jamaica, New York, has it and two hundred and twenty-five plus scientists and support staff with access to that toxin. The status of the police lab for the crime scene unit is uncertain, but any one of those two hundred and twenty-five mentioned could hand it off."

And Thomas, I think, which is a reason for me to visit his office and lab later tonight when he's gone. "I can try to narrow the list to those who have direct usage and access to the toxin," Tic Tac adds.

"In other words, everyone and their fucking uncle can get that toxin. Narrow it down. Find common denominators." I disconnect and head into the subway tunnel, on my way to the medical examiner's office, where I'm going to look at the medical examiner a little differently than in the past. That office might not have the chemical needed, but she has easy access to the main forensics operation that would. And Melanie is, after all, the woman who took over this case for Beth. And I now believe, who was part of a bigger picture. And not only does she have access to this investigation, she has Roger blabbing in her ear.

***

I exit the tunnel and dial Beth. She answers with a groan. "Lilah?"

"You were sleeping? Isn't it like eight pm there? Are you becoming your mother already?"

133

"Don't say crap like that to me, all right? I mean, damn it, Lilah. I'm having time change issues. What's happening?"

"Did you tell Melanie about the poison?"

"I tried. She hasn't returned my call. I called the reception area, and they said she isn't in the office."

"Don't tell her," I reply. "Not yet. Don't ask details. Go to bed or whatever."

"I left a detailed message for her, Lilah. Sorry."

"Of course, you did. You're a blurt it from the rooftops to save the world kind of person."

"Was that an insult?"

"You ask this because you think it's hard to tell when I'm trying to insult you?"

"I actually think you walk around insulting everyone, so yes. You were insulting me. Don't do that. I'm in another country, trying to help while fearing for my life."

"You have Kane's man and an ocean between you and this problem."

"Yes, well, Kane's man is wonderful, like really, really wonderful, Lilah. Like he's and we—"

"If you're about to tell me you're fucking him, right now, considering all I have going on, stop yourself."

"Oh. Right. Not a good time."

"Okay so now that we're passed that," I say. "Call me if Melanie calls you but don't talk to her." I hang up and turn the corner, bringing the medical examiner's building into view. Not that I'll be talking to Melanie. She's not in the office.

I'm not sure what to think about her being gone with three new autopsies and a serial killer to deal with. How does that even happen? Oh fuck. The same way Williams disappeared in the middle of an investigation. I stop walking and tab through my phone to find Melanie's number. She doesn't answer. I leave a message. "Call me now, Melanie." I don't want to scare her, but hell, fuck it. "I need a wellness check now."

Disconnecting, I decide that Melanie has fifteen minutes before I have Houston send a team to her house. I text her for good measure and get no reply. Her silence is worthy of attention. She might not be a victim, but Beth was headed in that direction. I start walking again and can't connect with real worry over Melanie. I'm feeling Melanie as an intentional replacement for Beth, rather than a victim. In which case, her time away is my time to play in her files. However, losing a detective and a medical examiner to the same killer would be a blow to the case and the city.

He likes that kind of attention.

CHAPTER TWENTY-SEVEN

I know my way around the medical examiner's facility and waste no time taking the stairs up several flights. Reaching the lab door, I test the knob to confirm it's locked. I then dig in my bag, pull out a tool I carry with me, one I bought from the shopper's network while eating strawberries and drinking some kind of Smore's martini recipe that inspired me to cook. Mixing a drink is cooking to me. It's an effort in the kitchen, which requires more than one ingredient. There might have been a voodoo doll, that looked like Kane, purchased that night, too, but I burned it, and the devil doesn't burn, so he was just fine.

The door is open in under twenty seconds, proving that booze and shopping are never bad, except that I'd bought a dress, too, thinking about Kane. Which is why I burned the doll. I enter the lab and shut the door, scanning for any sign of trouble that I don't find. Not that I'd likely find trouble here. Umbrella Man makes his victims' act of their own free, but manipulated will. For now, silence and an empty office is a ticket to me looking around, starting with Melanie's office, which appears to be in the back of the lab.

Hurrying that way, I enter, turn on the light and sit down behind the glossed wooden desk, pulling my small camera from my bag. I begin opening drawers and pulling out documents, shooting random pictures: bank accounts, memos, charity organizations, and much more. I'll analyze it all later. There's nothing on the drugs in inventory. There's a copy of her intake notes for the three victims, which, upon a cursory glance, appear basic and noneventful.

I think about the male DNA found at two of the crime scenes. If the killer is in forensics or law enforcement, he wouldn't leave that behind. That has to belong to someone working the case, someone who isn't the killer. Or the killer isn't connected to law enforcement at all, is not as smart as I think, and we're all stupid for not catching him yet.

I reject my own stupidity.

He, she, or them is connected to law enforcement.

I can't rule out a group funded by the Society, in which case, one stupid fool could fuck around and leave DNA, a "yes" man, who did more harm than good for the Umbrella Man persona. That feels right. God, I need to just sit down and put all these thoughts on cards. I search for an inventory of drugs in the lab but find nothing. I stand up to leave, and that's when I realize that Melanie has no personal items in her office. Not even her diploma. That reminds me of the first crime scene, though, last night, the soap star had personal items. Actually, no. She had Hollywood propaganda, which may or may not qualify as personal items.

I text Tic Tac: *Melanie Carmichael. She's the ME on this case. I need everything you can get me on her.*

I think of Beth who has family and isn't in entertainment. Beth isn't a typical victim, but she was in the way. She's my friend. I believe she was in danger.

I reach for Melanie's trashcan and grab a magazine. It's *Soap Opera Digest.* Is she reading about the victim rather than looking for the answers we need in an autopsy? Or did she buy this before she died? I bag it and shove it into my field bag.

Standing up, I plan to hunt down that inventory of chemicals on hand and then call for a wellness check as Roger steps into the doorway. "We should have shared a cab," he says, blocking the doorway, his piercing blue eyes meeting mine.

He wants me to explain why I didn't invite him. He can want away. "Do you know where she is?"

"Obviously, not in her office, but you are."

"Wellness check. She's not answering her calls or text messages."

"You should have just asked me. I was coming by to take her to lunch anyway."

He pulls his phone from his pocket and dials her number. He also stays in the doorway. He doesn't move. He's always played these power games when we were questioning people, which I get. I fuck my way into their heads. I do me. He does him. He's just not doing it to me. He never could. He knows that, too, and I'm not sure he likes it anymore than I've decided I like him. But then, like isn't really my thing.

"No answer," he says, putting his phone away. "Have you called downstairs to find out where she is?"

"I was told she's not in the building." I leave out Beth as my source. I want her out of the picture, though the fact that she's the one who discovered the toxin is going to be hard to do.

"Hello! Who's here? Hello?!"

"There she is," he says. "And you had her dead and in the morgue already."

That word "already" doesn't sit well, and I shove it down but not away for reasons I'll analyze later. Roger steps out of the room, and I round the desk. We greet Melanie, side by side, just outside her office. "Was my door unlocked?" she asks, shoving her hands in a lab coat. "Because I swear I locked it. There were reporters everywhere this morning."

"I unlocked it," I say. "Wellness check. You weren't answering your phone."

Her eyes go wide. "Wellness check?" She looks between me and Roger. "And yet, I'm not in danger?"

"It was a precaution," I say. "Why weren't you answering your phone?"

"I dropped my phone in a puddle last night. It won't work. My assistant is getting it replaced."

"The receptionist said you weren't even in the building," I reply.

"I came in early to do the autopsies," she explains. "Before she arrived. I couldn't sleep. You know I watched Karen on two different soaps growing up. Katy's the spitting image of her. Twins are always quite incredible that way."

In other words, she could have picked up *Soap Opera Digest* this morning, reliving those memories. But why throw it away?

She looks between us again. "I hate that I made you both rush over here."

"Roger came for your lunch date," I comment.

She frowns. "Date?" She glances at Roger. "We have a date?"

"Lunch," Roger amends, offering nothing more.

"Oh well, I can't," she says, sounding frazzled. "I need to get my reports done for law enforcement." She touches his arm. "But you know I'd love to go. I love our little chats."

Little chats.

Roger chats?

Maybe at you but not with you. If she managed to change that, she has mad skills, but I'm not here to ponder his dictatorial breakdown. "I need to head out," I say on that note. "What do I need to know before the reports are ready?"

"I don't have much to offer but confirmation of the crime scene data," she says, turning her attention to me. "The two women with umbrellas were posed and poisoned. Detective Williams was not. She was shot, as was one of the woman who was in the alleyway with her, but she was poisoned as well."

"That woman" is the soap opera star she just beamed about and called by name, which is interesting. The name usage is more common when the speaker knew the deceased but then some people really start thinking they know television personalities. Maybe she's that kind of freak.

"The bullets were in the hearts, placed with precision," she continues. "Those are not easy shots to make in the dark and rain."

"Sounds like a highly skilled marksman," Roger interjects. "Law enforcement or military."

Because it was *Ghost*.

And this conversation is a reminder of how easily he could put a bullet in Kane's heart. That asshole needs to take that threat more seriously.

"There's not much else," Melanie adds quickly, saving me any further discussion about those assassinations. "No DNA this time. The rain damage was just too extensive. Of course, the blood from the ceiling fan, as you might guess, was once again pigs' blood. I'm afraid we're still struggling to find that toxin."

Melanie could be the Society, and once they know we're getting close, they'll end this. They'll come for me and Kane before we can come for them. They could come for Beth. "Beth thought she found the toxin," I say, launching into a lie like a chip off my politician father's shoulder. "She left you a message, but she was mistaken." It's out. It's spoken. Now I just need to get to Beth before she does. And hope like hell she didn't leave the name of the toxin in that message.

Melanie's brow furrows. "That's odd," she says. "I'll call her. Maybe she's closer than she thinks. If you'll both excuse me, I need to call from my office." She gives a laugh. "Forced into using a landline. How did we survive without cellphones?" And, with that, she walks away.

"Why do you suppose he shot the one who was poisoned?" Roger asks.

"To save me from the booby traps."

He's not done asking, "Then why set them?"

"To show off his skills and taunt me with what comes next."

"And what comes next, Lilah?"

A drink, I think, and maybe a few voodoo dolls. Voodoo dolls are underrated.

"I'm coming down with you," Melanie says, rushing back into the lab with her purse on her shoulder. "My assistant can't get my phone. They won't give it to her."

I end up in the hallway with her and Roger. They head to the elevator. With no explanation, I head for the stairs.

"Oh wait. Agent Love!" At Melanie's shout, I breathe out and then turn.

"There's something I didn't mention. It may be nothing." She and Roger step closer to me. Her brow furrows, and her voice lowers. "I'll just tell you, and you can figure out if it matters. Karen had cigarette burns on her fingers. It was as if she held the cigarette until it burned down and into her skin. Per her lungs and the Internet, she wasn't a smoker."

It's another message, and my eyes meet Roger's and he says, "You still think this has nothing to do with me?" he challenges.

I step to him. "Are you telling me you're the killer, Roger?"

"Do you think I'm the killer, Lilah?"

"I think you're an asshole, Roger. You know that was a threat. You know what he was telling me."

"Tell me. What was he telling you?"

"Eventually, he's going to kill the people close to me and then kill me."

"That's right," he agrees. "That's exactly what he's telling you."

CHAPTER TWENTY-EIGHT

Roger's a dick. He's always been a dick. He will always be a dick.

Lord help me, I'm the bitch version of him minus the ego. His fucking ego is literally going to be the death of him.

"You're right," I say. "This is about you. What better way for him to prove that he's better than me than by killing my mentor?"

"Mentor and protégé," he says. "That's what you think this is about?"

"Yes. Don't be an asshole and a stubborn old fool," I bite out. "Leave town before you end up dead."

"I've conquered too many killers to walk away now," he says, arrogance radiating off of him. "I'm staying. I'm helping, whether you like it or not. He wants me to. He *wants* me to."

"And you yourself told me to never give them what they want."

"You're what he wants," he says. "Not me. Isn't that what you keep saying? I'm not giving him what he wants. I'm giving him me."

"You're a means to an end."

"I'm not leaving, Lilah."

"Then you better hope I work faster than him." I turn and head for the stairwell.

The minute the door is shut, I pull out my phone and dial Beth. She answers with, "Did you find her? Did you talk to Melanie? Is she okay?"

"She's fine. Did you tell her the toxin's name in the voicemail?"

"No. No, I didn't. I thought when she called—"

"Then here is your story. You made a mistake. Samples got mixed up. You didn't find the toxin. And don't bring up the correct toxin. Don't let anyone know that's on our radar."

"Why? What is this, Lilah? You're scaring me. What don't I know?"

"It's what I don't know that's the issue. I don't know who's behind this yet," I say, "but there's a high probability, they're in law enforcement. That means they could have access to the investigation. I don't want whoever this is to know that we're getting closer."

"You don't trust Melanie?"

"Not only do I not know her, but that facility where she's working at is well-stocked with that chemical, or whatever the fuck it is, you identified. That means the killer could be close to her. It could be her. We don't know."

"Melanie?"

"I'm just telling you that we don't know who did this, and I'm sure you know there were three more victims."

"Yes. I heard."

"Which proves my point," I say. "Information travels in law enforcement circles. And I want to keep your name out of this. Just don't tell anyone. No one. Say it, Beth."

"Okay. I won't tell anyone."

"Good. I need to go."

"Oh Lord, this is bad," she groans. "You told me you were hanging up. You never tell me you're hanging up. You're trying to make me feel better. You. Lilah Love. Are trying to comfort me."

I'm not comforting her. I don't do comfort. I hang up and text Zar: *Leaving. Front door. Headed home.*

He can keep up or not. That's on him. If he can't, I don't need him. If he can, he might be a resource. If he pulls a stunt like Jay, I might kill him myself.

I exit the stairwell to the lobby, and I don't pause. I don't need another Roger encounter. Thank fuck, I'm outside in a few minutes flat, thunder rumbling above, threatening to drench me, but I push forward, turning right toward the apartment. I could, and probably should, take a car, but screw the rain. Screw Umbrella Man. Screw my father for getting us all waist-deep in shit. And right now, I need to think. I need to figure shit out. I need to catch this asshole, and I need to understand what I'm feeling, which is nothing.

I am *not* worried about Roger. His meddling is irritating, yes, but I don't fear him being hurt. My God, what is wrong with me? He's my mentor. He did a lot to move my career forward, and I owe him, but I feel no fear for him. I feel no worry. I warned him. He's the fool who won't listen, and it pisses me off. That's all I feel: pissed off. Since I stabbed that man, I've slowly felt those emotional chips flip off.

The crowds push and shove, and I cut through to an alleyway that leads to another street I need to reach. I hope Umbrella Man is watching. Bring it. Bring it on. Fuck with me right now and lose. I walk with an even, calculated pace, waiting for my emotions to show themselves, willing them to show the fuck up. Halfway down the alleyway, it starts to freaking rain. A black SUV pulls in front of my path to exit. It stops there.

Obviously, it's waiting for me.

I don't stop walking. It could be Kane. It could be the monster I'm hunting. Let it be him. My hand settles on my weapon, and I walk faster, confrontation in the air. Anger burns through me. That's one emotion that's never wavered. It's my friend. It's the bitch I will happily call family because it doesn't control me. I control it. And I'm in the mood to end this here and now. I draw nearer. The SUV idles in place. I charge right at the back door, and the window rolls down revealing Kane inside.

"Don't shoot me," he says, his eyes twinkling with mischief, his gaze flicking to my hand on my weapon, before returning to my face. "Then you'll have to sleep alone because I swear Lilah fucking Love, I'll crawl out of the grave and kill any asshole who thinks he can replace me." He pops the door open.

"You asshole," I growl, holstering my weapon and stepping into the opening he's created for me. "Call me. Warn me. Stop stalking me."

"Get in, beautiful," he orders, and the fact that his driver gets out of the vehicle, umbrella in hand, tells me he has something to say that couldn't be said by phone.

I get in and shut the door, intending to cuss him out, but as I shut myself inside and I turn to look at him, that's not what happens. That bond between us mixes with the danger lighting up our lives right now, and the anger fades. "Why are you here?" I say.

"It's raining," he says. "He likes the rain, and I love you. I'm here *for you.*"

Just like that, emotions pierce my chest. He's here for me. No one is ever here for me, but Kane. He's worried about me. I'm worried about him. I'm gutted at the idea of Ghost killing him. Kane makes me *feel.* He keeps me human and all those "I needs" that went through my mind while walking are nothing. He's the only real need there is for me.

The next thing I know I'm climbing onto his lap, straddling him, pressing my hands to his face. "Lilah?"

"Kane," I whisper, my mouth lowering until I'm kissing him, proving to myself I'm right. I feel with this man. I'm human with this man. I am not a monster, too.

A low sound escapes his throat, and his hand settles on the back of my head. He is all in, kissing the hell out of me, but he's not in control. It's me. I drive the passion, I demand more. I need Kane Mendez, and I don't even care who or what he is. I've been wrong to act as if it does, as if that part of him is what drags me to hell. He's the reason I'm not there yet.

Rain begins to pound on the roof, and Kane catches my hair, pulling my lips from his. "What is this, Lilah?"

"Kiss me again." I press my lips to his, and he does, he kisses me, but I also land on my back, with him leaning over me. "I know you," he says, tearing his mouth from mine. "What's wrong? What's going on?"

He knows me. He does. And he thinks the badge belongs on my person. He thinks I'm a better person than I am. Or maybe he doesn't. Maybe he just believes it's the badge and together that keeps us both human. Because he knows how close we both walk to hell.

"Talk to me," he orders.

"After we fuck and I spend about two hours in Purgatory."

He leans in and kisses me. "After we fuck," he says, his voice low and rough. "Before Purgatory." He doesn't wait for an answer. He sits up, takes me with him, and then knocks on the window. The driver with his umbrella climbs inside. I leave the order of events as he's stated them alone but not because I plan to bend to his will. Because right now, there is a dark clawing at my mind, that part of me that felt nothing with Roger, trying to push past everything Kane just made me feel, trying to talk to me. I refuse to listen.

Kane catches my leg and holds me close, and that dark clawing eases, thank God. There's something combustible about this man, this vehicle, and the rain. If only it didn't feel like it was raining blood.

CHAPTER TWENTY-NINE

The ride is short and silent.

The driver drops us at the door, where there are barriers and security set up, because, Jesus, there's press everywhere. We enter the building to find Kit behind the desk, but he's also got about ten people around him. Clearly, the tenants aren't happy. I'm sure they expect the building management to assure them no one dies here. Some people have really unrealistic expectations.

I, for one, just want out of the lobby and into the privacy of our apartment. Kane seems to feel the same way; his strides are as long as mine. We aren't holding hands. We don't do the hand holding thing in public. Okay, there are moments, but, right now, we're both all about getting the fuck into the elevator and up to the seventeenth floor.

We step into the car, and Kit is suddenly holding the door. He hands me a CD. "That's the security footage for the building. I've watched it ten times. The sister, Katy, comes in and out of the building several times in forty-eight hours. No one else. I have thoughts on that I don't want to say here where we're on camera." He backs up and lets the door shut.

I shove the CD in my bag, and my mind goes where I think his did. Karen, our soap opera star, killed her sister and then left, only to be killed herself. But how would Umbrella Man make her kill her sister? Who would she want to save more than her sister? It makes no sense, and yet, it feels like that's the only way this happened. Unless Karen didn't think the drug would kill her. That has to be it.

The car starts to move, and Kane glances over at me. He's going where I'm going. I see it in his eyes. This building's secure. Umbrella Man had to use the sister to kill the other sister in order to pull this off. We're secure here, and that makes me think about why he's not at work. He came for me to bring me back here. I'm back to the thought I forgot—the driver got out of the car. Kane came to protect me, I believe that, maybe, he just came to convince me to go home. But there was something else, something he wanted to say to me, something he thought would convince me to go home with him.

Or, maybe it was just the fucking rain.

We're being conditioned to fear the rain.

Even the fierce Kane Mendez.

A few beats later, we exit the car, and after a brief walk, we step to our door, the door that was once ours and is now ours again. We live together, and I'm done, really done, with regrets. The agency can't come at Kane forever. They're after him now because he dared to sue them. Because he dared to back them off. I have thoughts on that, thoughts on how the agency clearly wants to use Kane, but for now, I set them aside. Kane's opened the door, and I walk inside the foyer.

I'm just entering the main apartment when the doorbell rings behind us. My cellphone rings as well, and the two of us share a frustrated look. We divide, him heading to the door and me heading further into the apartment, snaking my phone from my bag as I do, to find Tic Tac's number. "What do you have for me?" I ask, heading up the stairs.

"Your email is locked and loaded," he says. "I've sent you a small library of documents, but I've included a summary of my findings and what I think you might want to look at first." He covers the phone, but I hear. "This is my job. Don't do this right now."

"Oh hell," I say, dropping my bag on the floor by my nightstand and sitting down on the unmade bed, the storm darkening the room and forcing me to flip on the light. "I don't care how hot your new boyfriend is, if he's already bitching about your job, he's gotta go. Because, you know, he'll bitch and then cheat and blame your work. Then you'll be crying. You won't be able to do your job. Murphy will fire you. I'll have to train someone new to work my way."

"Jesus, Lilah. Really?"

"Just saving the world two people at a time. That's you and me, Tic Tac."

"I'd hang up, but you'll punish me in some Lilah Love way, and I also have more to say."

"More to say. Well, by all means, say more."

"Melanie Carmichael. She's from a stable family, three siblings—two sisters who are both family doctors in Jersey. They're in practice together. She was married for fifteen years, but her husband died of a heart attack. The interesting part is that her brother is a surgeon who works at NYC General. He donated to your father's campaign. He also attended several campaign events with Pocher. Based on the guest lists, Houston and Roger have been at some of the same events."

And Roger was used to get me to the first crime scene. The minute I came back to New York and became a problem again, they decided to use my history with him, to pull me into this case and get rid of me. "I need a list of everyone who was at any event Roger was at."

"You got it. And Murphy wants you to call him."

"Murphy can call me if he needs me." My phone beeps with a message. I glance at it.

"It's Murphy, right?" Tic Tac asks.

"Yes, smartass." I disconnect and make the call. "Director Murphy."

"The mayor called me."

"And?"

"You tell me."

"It's a familiar problem, a cloak and dagger situation."

"Them," he says, and I know he means the Society.

"Yes. Them. I'm handling it. I have resources. That's why you hired me, right?" I'm talking about Kane.

He knows, too. He doesn't miss a beat. "I hired you for you, Lilah. But remember this. They are everywhere. One falls, another rises. Finesse. Fuck them, but with finesse. That's all for now." He hangs up.

Kane enters the room, a large envelope in his hand. He crosses toward me, and I stand to face him. He stops in front of me and hands it to me. "What is it?"

"The delivery that just came for me. Look inside."

I open it and eye three disposable phones. I glance up at him, the question I don't ask in my eyes. "Was there a note?"

"There doesn't need to be a note. I put the word out that I wanted to reach Ghost. He expected it after last night, which is why he reacted quickly. This was his answer. He'll call."

Ice radiates down my spine. "Ghost," I repeat, that empty spot where I should keep all those emotions I do not, filling up. "What are you going to do?"

"Give him a new job."

He means kill Pocher. "Murphy said when one falls, another rises. I know you know that or you would have done this before now."

"I've shown extreme restraint by not killing him thus far. It's time everyone in the damn Society knows when one falls, another can fall."

"And if Ghost has an agreement with Pocher, too?"

"Ghost knows I'll double any offer. Ghost knows I have his back. That's why he saved you."

He has the back of an assassin. It's one of those moments when I should be appalled, but I'm not. I toss the envelope on the bed and grab his tie, yanking him toward me. "I don't trust him, Kane."

"You've said that. You're going to have to trust me."

"Have to? I don't fucking have to do anything."

"You don't trust me, Lilah?"

"Don't twist the meaning of my words to justify your cavalier actions. To be clear, I trust you, but I think you forget that you're human."

"I told you. I've got this."

"And if you don't?"

"I do. Let it go. Let me—"

"Let me make this clear, Kane Mendez of the Mendez family, if you think the wrath of your family is bad, you don't know me. If this goes wrong. If he kills you, I'll live just to kill him. It'll come down to him and me. Do you want it to come down to him and me?"

His hands slide under my hair, and he drags me to him. "It will always come down to you and me, Lilah. Always."

His mouth closes down on mine, and if I wanted emotion, I have emotion. I have too many emotions. I can't escape them. For right now, I don't want to escape them. I'm angry at Kane. I'm afraid of him dying, and I don't feel fear. And the only way I have to deal with those things is *with him.*

CHAPTER THIRTY

My anger is in my kiss, in the way I shove at his jacket. It's in every movement that lands us naked and on the bed, but there is more to what I feel. There is unfamiliar desperation. I can't touch him enough. I can't get him inside me fast enough. When he finally is, I press him to the mattress, and I'm on top, wanting to bend him to my will like that is even possible with this man. I want to make him be rational. I want to make him stay, but some part of me can't make that clawing sensation go away.

Kane rolls me to my back and presses my hands to the mattress on either side of me. "Stop fucking kissing me like this is goodbye, woman. It's never goodbye for us. Never again. Never, Lilah."

"You—"

"Love you. I love you so fucking much that, yes, I would kill for you. Yes, I will bury a million bodies for you. And yes, I will bleed for you, but I'm doing it all right here with you." He lowers his mouth to mine and brushes his lips over mine. "We do this, all of it, together. Say it."

"Kane—"

"*Say it,* Lilah."

"Together. But you better remember that and not get killed. You better—"

He brushes his lips over mine and smiles against my mouth. "You can never just agree, can you?"

"I'm never going to be that girl."

"Good. I bet if I asked you to marry me again, you'd say 'yes, but' to that, too."

My chest tightens, damn these emotions. "Kane," I whisper.

"Lilah," he whispers, and then he's kissing me again, and at some point, my hands are free, and I'm free with him. What I feel is no longer desperate but something softer, and I am never soft. Except with him. With Kane, perhaps, I'm

155

human because he allows me to be all the things that I am. And when we're lying together, in the darkness, listening to the rain, I flashback to that night on the beach. I flashback to me in that shower covered in blood. I flashback to him being there. We're bonded in the very blood that once separated us.

"What was all of this about?" he asks, rolling us to our sides to face each other.

I sit up and curl my knees to my chest, withdrawing, but that withdrawal is about me, not him. He grabs his shirt and wraps it around me before he tugs on his pants. Somehow, he knew I needed boundaries, and he's confident enough in himself and us, to not find that intimidating. He settles back on the mattress, and his hand rests on my knees.

I tell him everything I've discovered, my reasons for keeping the toxin secret, and finally, those cigarette burns that lead to a threat against Roger. "I told him to leave town. He won't."

His eyes narrow. "And?"

I press my hands to my face and then scoot off the bed to stand up, pacing the room. Kane moves to sit on my side of the mattress. I pace some more and turn to face him. "A lot of times, I don't feel what I should feel, Kane. You know that, right?"

"What does that mean?" he asks cautiously.

"Roger is being stupid. He's going to die. I actually thought—okay, you want to be a fool. Die a fool. I felt no remorse. I don't feel those things. I've always had that in me, but after my attack—"

He's suddenly standing in front of me, his hands on my shoulders. "You sent Beth away. You worried for Beth. You put her in the damn Ritz to protect her. You held back the toxin to protect her. You fight every day for people who died because you care. Stop making yourself the monster, Lilah. You are not the monster."

"But—"

"You are not the monster. You've got your Otherworld for a reason. It's your way of shutting off your emotions. It's sanity."

"And you? Is that what you do?"

His expression tightens. "I'm not you."

"What does that even mean?"

"I don't need an Otherworld to shut things out, beautiful. You know that, even if you try to pretend it's not true." He cups my face. "A badge wouldn't shut me down. The badge on you shuts me down. Stop fighting who you are."

"Roger—"

"You don't feel nothing. That's not what this is." He releases me and folds his arms in front of his chest, studying me. "You're blocking out what you feel, just like you do when you go to a crime scene and mentally step into your Otherworld. What are you blocking out?"

My brows furrow. "I don't—I'm not."

"You are," he says as if it's just simply a fact. "I know you. You absolutely are." He kisses me, a tender act that, in itself, defies his declared coldness. The warmth I feel with it defies mine. "I'm going to throw on some jeans and order us a pizza," he says. "That's your preferred thinking food."

"Hell's Kitchen," I murmur, as he walks into the bathroom to get to the closet.

I stand there a minute, processing what he's just said. I'm suppressing emotion rather than not feeling it at all. Am I? I dress, replaying that encounter with Roger and Melanie, looking for answers. I've just finished dressing when one of the phones in that envelope, the one that is still somehow on the bed, rings. Ghost is calling. Good. He and I need to have another little chat.

CHAPTER THIRTY-ONE

"Hello, Ghost," I answer.

"Lilah," he says, and he doesn't sound surprised. "Always a pleasure. Do you have a name for me?"

"I told you, if I had a name, I'd kill him myself. Do *you* have a name?"

"No, but he's a sick fuck. I told you. I'll kill him for free."

"*He's a sick fuck?*"

"He does it for pleasure. For you and me, it's business."

"I do it to protect people. You do it for money."

"You need to justify it. One day, you'll get over that."

Kane appears in the doorway in black jeans and a black long sleeve T-shirt, looking so damn arrogantly Kane Mendez, that I know I haven't gotten through to him. "If you kill Kane," I say to Ghost, "it'll be all kinds of personal for me, and you will no longer be the best assassin on the planet. I will be, and you'll be dead. And I'll enjoy killing you."

Kane is in front of me now, taking the phone. I let him. I've said what I needed to say. "Ghost," he greets, and then eyes me, amusement in his stare, in the quirk of his lips. "Yes. Yes, she is." He listens a moment and says, "Time-sensitive." Another pause. "When?" And then. "Yes." He disconnects.

"What was that?" I demand.

"We do these things in person, Lilah."

"You can't meet him. He'll kill you."

"He's not going to kill me."

"I will shoot you in the damn leg before you go meet him."

He catches my hip and walks me to him. "I love you, too."

"Kane—"

"I know what I'm doing. You want transparency, Lilah. This is it. I could have pretended that was someone else. I would have pretended that was someone else in the past."

I inhale on that and turn away from him, before facing him again. He's right. I asked for this. If I fight his every move, he'll stop telling me the truth. "And yet, you didn't want to tell me how you're handling Pocher."

"I thought a lot about that today," he says. "You're right. I promised you that I'd stop shutting you out. I'm not doing that now, but I hope like hell we both don't regret that."

I sit down on the bed, making sure he knows that I'm not running. "You're going to have Ghost kill Pocher?" It's obvious, of course, but I want confirmation.

He sits down next to me. "And make it look like Umbrella Man did it. It's not a far reach after he delivered that pig to a Pocher-sponsored event."

"He doesn't kill men."

"I know that, Lilah."

My heart thunders in my ears. "Who else is he going to kill?"

"I need your cousin to connect him to one of the victims."

This answer delivers relief. Kane isn't going to kill someone just to cover up Pocher's murder. I know him. I know this man, and suddenly, transparency isn't going to prove me wrong. "It's there already. Several of them donated to my father's campaign. I can connect the dots to link Pocher. I just haven't figured out how they're picking who Umbrella Man kills."

"Whoever is behind the murders can't talk. We can't let Umbrella Man tell his story. He can't be arrested. He has to die."

"Don't expect me to object. I won't."

"You understand what knowing these things means for you, right? You understand the liability?"

"We can't be us, and you live two lives, Kane."

"If anything ever comes back on me, you deny ever knowing anything. Promise me. Promise me that you'll protect yourself."

"Kane—"

"Promise me or I just told you the last thing I will ever tell you that crosses a line."

"Damn it," I curse, squeezing my eyes shut. "Fine. Yes. I promise." I look at him. "I promise."

He studies me a few beats and then says, "You're going to kill Ghost and enjoy it?"

My lips curve. "What did he say about that?"

"That you're a badass. I agreed." His words are light, but there is something else there, something hesitant, something hard. "What aren't you saying?"

"There's more. There's something I need to tell you, and you aren't going to like it."

CHAPTER THIRTY-TWO

I fight the urge to stand up and face him, but that's confrontational, and we're on new ground here. He's talking to me. This is what I asked for. "I'm listening," I say.

"I made some calls about the poison."

My heart starts to thunder in my ears, and I blurt out, "Beth found out what the poison is."

Words I've already spoken when I hate repeaters. Repeaters are usually liars, trying to validate a lie. In my case, some part of me is giving him a reason to stop now, before he goes too far.

"But what you don't know," he says, "is where Umbrella Man got that poison."

"It would be a lab or a facility that makes paint or varnish. It's—"

His hand comes down on my leg. That touch and the intensity rolling off of him silences me. "I made some calls," he repeats. "My uncle's *'company'* takes special requests for a hefty fee. He filled an order for barium acetate."

My breath lodges in my throat, and I push it out. "You supplied the drugs that killed all the victims?"

"Not me, Lilah. I am not involved in what he does."

I stand up and face him now. "And yet, it was you who just went and calmed a war the cartel was about to erupt inside."

He stands up. "And you know the internal battle I had with the idea that I would have to take over, but you know me. Do you think I'd let that happen?"

"I guess this is the elephant in the room for us, Kane. Drugs kill people all the time. Drugs that *your family* sells."

"I don't want to be a part of this fucking world my father created, Lilah. You know that, like no one knows that. But they keep coming at me. They keep *fucking* coming. You were wrong when you said I can't live two lives. I have no choice. You say you want to know about those lives. You say

163

you want to be a part of them. Well, here's your chance to change your mind. This can be it. From this point forward, you don't have to know."

"I've always known. Pretending I don't has always divided us."

"We feel pretty damn divided now, Lilah."

I shove a hand through my hair and grab my bag, "I just need to think right now. I need to figure out how to fix all of this."

"*You* need to fix it, Lilah? Just you? Not me? Not us?"

"No. Yes. I *need* to go to Purgatory."

"Right." His lips thin, voice hard. "Go to Purgatory." He heads toward the bedroom door and disappears into the hallway, thunder rumbling the windows in his aftermath.

I turn and walk into Purgatory, sit down on the floor and pull out my computer, the *Soap Opera Digest*, and a stack of paperwork. I then grab the notecards and set them in front of me, but I do nothing but stare at them. Literally, stare at them. I have a million things pounding at my mind, and I want to talk to Kane about them. I want to talk to Kane. I never talk to anyone but that man, and I can say anything to him. And I just made him feel like he can't talk to me. And, holy fuck. I stand up. Did he leave? Did he go to meet Ghost? No. No, he couldn't have left like this.

I take off out of the room, and I don't stop until I'm on the stairs and shouting, "Kane?! Kane?!" I charge down the stairs as he rounds the corner to the kitchen.

I close the space between us and stop dead in my tracks, and damn it, I'm breathing hard. "I thought you went to meet Ghost."

His expression softens. The only time Kane Mendez softens is for me. That means something. "Not until seven, after dark."

My hands go to his chest. "I need you to figure out how to fix all of this. I need *you*, Kane."

He drags me to him and kisses me. "And I, Lilah, need you."

"Then don't go meet Ghost."

"I'm going to meet Ghost."

"I'll go with you," I counter.

"No."

"Kane—"

"No, Lilah. For ten reasons, including your badge—no."

He's a wall of words. He's not going to take me. I know the battles I can win. I won't win this one. "Then kill him before he kills you."

"If it comes to that, I will. I'm always ready." The doorbell rings. "Pizza," he says. "And a conversation about Roger in Purgatory."

"Roger?"

"Yes. We never finished talking about Roger. I think we should."

LISA RENEE JONES

CHAPTER THIRTY-THREE

Kane and I are quick to sit down on the floor of Purgatory, with our favorite chairs at our backs. We don't immediately talk about Roger. For just a few minutes, we take a timeout and eat our damn pizza. A slice in, I ask, "Anything more on Jay?"

"The same," he says. "I told him to get well so I can kill him for acting like a scared little bitch who was afraid of me."

I laugh because he's joking. "He wasn't scared, not of what was in the alleyway. He was too damn much of a hero."

"Who overreacted because he was scared of me."

"Hmmm," I finish off a slice while Kane does the same. "Why is that I wonder?"

"I'm good to the people who work for me."

"Until they screw up," I counter.

"Letting you get hurt would be more than a screw-up."

"I can take care of myself." I grab another slice and shift the topic. "What about Roger?"

He shuts the pizza box and shoves his plate in a trashcan. "He gets under your skin. He always has."

"He was my mentor," I argue. "I was learning from him, and he wanted fast results. Every second that I let pass, that a killer is free, is a chance for him to kill again. That's my life. He was preparing me for that."

He angles in my direction. "There you go. He put that on you. Do it now, figure it out now, or someone dies. That's a big load to carry."

"It's part of the job."

"He made you feel like a damn killer, Lilah."

"Roger didn't do that."

"He mentally had you in a place that set you up for where you landed emotionally after your attack."

"My attack alone did that to me."

"No," he insists. "You'd come home from working with him, frustrated, unable to figure out a case."

"I was learning."

"You had a mental block with that man. Once you were home, in Purgatory, once you were in your own head, *you* solved the cases. Not me. Not him. He didn't make you better, and he's not making you better now."

I pull a knee to my chest, thinking what I felt in that lab earlier. "You're right. I felt that today when I was with him. There was something in my mind, and I just couldn't reach in and pull it out. I still don't know what it was. It's like I have flipping daddy issues with that man. And with my own father, who didn't even call after last night, and you know he knows what happened. He's running for office in New York City."

"Roger and your father. The only two people in this world I've ever seen fuck with your head."

"And you," I say. "You did, too."

"Your issue was not with me, but my name and what it represents. And it never stopped you from telling me to fuck off or putting me in my place."

I snort. "Like that's possible."

"You sure as hell think you can."

"*Think?*" I challenge.

He doesn't take the bait, pulling me back to his point. "With them, you hold back, Lilah."

"Daddy issues," I concede again. "I get it. And apparently, so does the Society, since they used Roger to get me to the first crime scene, and Umbrella Man pulled the pig stunt at my father's event." I frown. "That was to screw with my head and get him press." A bitter taste touches my tongue. "You saved me before they killed me after my attack. You denied them the sympathy votes they wanted for my father. They have to make them up now." A vacuum of history starts to suck me under. Does my father know they intend to kill us? "God, I really do have daddy issues." I try to get up.

Kane catches my arm. "Lilah—"

"Do not even *think* about fucking coddling me, Kane Mendez. I need to work. I need to find them. I need to kill all of these bastards. And I can bury my own bodies this time."

His eyes darken. "Can I get you a shovel or some coffee?"

And just like that, my boiling point, which is at about an eight, rachets down to a four, and I laugh. "No shovel yet, but coffee would be *lovely*. See, since you're being all proper and polite, I can say something other than fuck. And you can throw some manpower in my direction, too. I can't use anyone in law enforcement."

He releases me. "Get Kit details on whatever you need. He'll make it happen. What else?"

My mind is back on Kane's observation about Roger. "Roger keeps saying this is about him. I think they're using his ego against him and me."

"Meaning what?"

I stand up, and he moves to sit in the chair. I start to pace, pulling my thought all the way through, before I explain. "Roger has a thing for the new medical examiner who I've linked to the Society. Her brother works at a hospital that stocks barium, which is why I thought he might have supplied the drugs."

His lips tighten. "He didn't."

"I know. I get it. I stepped in shit on that one, but that's not the point. She was at a few events with Roger. They must have seen his interest in her. They also knew that if they involved him in this case, which explains the cigarette they left at the first crime scene, they needed to pull him into the investigation, so he'd know what I was doing on the case. They wanted to scare Beth away so that they could bring in Melanie and use her to extract information from him."

"To keep tabs on you."

"Exactly."

"And most everything I just said is unproven, but damn good in theory. If I'm right, and I believe I am, they won't kill him until they don't need him. Until they're done with us."

"Until we're done with them," Kane amends. "And that's soon."

"Which is why I need to find Umbrella Man. Who could be more than one person, by the way. Or, one person with Society helpers. That feels more on point, but it could also be why we don't catch one familiar person on security feeds." I grab my MacBook from the floor and sit down behind my desk, snagging paper to begin making a list of everyone I need watched for safety reasons or otherwise, as well as everything I need someone to follow up on. I then email Tic Tac to have him add addresses, names and critical information. The list is long and includes a trip to the pig farm. I know Houston had someone go check out the closest locations at one point but there is something to be found there, something missed. I'm all but done when I blink as Kane sets a cup of coffee and a bag of chocolate in front of me, my thinking tools. I didn't even know he'd left the room.

"It's not spiked, but we can fix that," he says.

"No booze until we're done with them. Thank you," I add, reaching for my cup. "See? Still being polite."

"Well, we both know you know how to say please," he says then winks.

I laugh because he's being dirty. God, I do love a dirty Kane Mendez. "I don't remember that word choice ever." I sip my coffee and set it down and move on before he details a particular moment when I did, in fact, say please, which he might. "I have the list. How do I get it to Kit?"

"I'll take it."

I scoot around in my chair, pull it off the printer behind me and then hand it to him. "You still have someone watching Lily, right?" I ask. "Because she's intimately involved with a man who was dating Williams. I still believe she could end up a victim."

"Yes," he confirms. "Nothing unusual, but I can have the man watching her text you." He glances at the list he's now holding. "You don't have Roger on the list."

I frown and grab the list. "I do." I scan for his name. It's not there. "I swear it's like I want him to end up dead. I meant to include him. I think I thought we were already watching him."

He studies me a few beats, and then says, "I'll add him."

He moves to his seat and sits down, where his own MacBook is waiting on the table next to it, with a cup of his own. Of course, while studying me, he'd been trying to figure out where my head is on Roger. And where the fuck *is* my head on Roger? Why did I leave him off the list? What is wrong with me? The Society is watching him. They threatened him. I should want Kane to watch over him. I'm about to go down the emotionless bitch killer profiler rabbit hole, which won't get my job done, so I shake off those thoughts and text Houston: *DNA samples. Where are we?*

You really want to do this to law enforcement? he replies.

My response is two words: *Yes. Now.*

He doesn't reply, but I can almost feel him cursing. Satisfied that I'll make him a foul mouth sailor yet, I move on. I open up Tic Tac's reports and start writing the names of everyone who was at the crime scenes on their own notecard. I'm about five in when Kane's phone rings, and he stands up and walks out of the room. I sip my coffee and realize that this is the first time I don't wonder what he's hiding when he does that. He knows and is on good terms with my demons. It's time I know his, though, I don't think he wants me on good terms. I think just the opposite. I think we're both in trouble when that happens.

I glance down at my notecards and the CSI guy who was taking pictures in the alleyway last night pops in my head. Mitch was his name. I look through the cards that I've made from Tic Tac's list. He's not here. Name. What was his last name? Mitch. Mitch McAllen, that's it. I dial Tic Tac. "You need stuff," he answers, "I know."

"Finally, you're getting the hang of this. There was a Mitch McAllen on the CSI team last night. I don't see him on your list."

"If he was there, he's on my list, but hold on. Let me look him up." His fingers tap the keyboard, and I sip my coffee as several sighs and more key tapping occurs on his end. I put him on speaker, to work while he works, and Kane chooses then to walk into the room.

I point to the phone. "Tic Tac," I say.

"I'm trying, Lilah," Tic Tac snaps.

I scowl at the phone. "That's very disrespectful, and you're on speakerphone."

"Oh God," he groans. "Tell me Murphy isn't there."

Kane arches a brow and sits down. I furrow mine. "Is Murphy here?"

"He said he was headed that way."

And he didn't tell me? I don't like where that's leading. "Great," I murmur. "Go ahead and shoot me."

"He listens to this recorded line, Lilah," Tic Tac says.

"You let him listen to your cellphone?" I challenge, because, of course, he doesn't.

Kane laughs, and Tic Tac groans, "Oh God," again. "Is that—is that Kane?"

"Yes, Tic Tac," Kane confirms, amusement lighting his brown eyes. "I'll send someone right over to kill you, too. Can I have the address?"

Tic Tac gives a choked laugh. "You're funny. He's funny. He's joking, right, Lilah?"

"Mitch McAllen, Tic Tac. Focus."

"There is no Mitch McAllen on the CSI team or with the department at all. I even checked contractors. He doesn't exist."

CHAPTER THIRTY-FOUR

"Is it him? Is he the killer?" Tic Tac asks.

"No." I glance at Kane who arches a brow in challenge. "Maybe," I concede. "I need you to go through the security feed and find the CSI guy taking photos. Send me that footage."

"There's no footage in the alleyway itself," he says. "And I didn't see him. The first footage we have is a block away."

"Holy fuck! I do not have time for this," I grind out. "Look for the CSI jacket. Mid-forties with a salt and pepper beard. And pale green eyes that stand out."

"I'll do what I can," he says. "But—"

"Do better, Tic Tac. People are dead. More are going to be dead." I hang up and look at Kane. "I just did to him what you said Roger did to me, right?"

"That man is never going to believe he's a killer."

"That statement says something about me that I'll analyze later." I pick up my phone from the desk and consider my next move. "I need to know if Houston knows this guy."

"But?" Kane prods.

"What if he's a part of this? What if he's Umbrella Man, and this says I'm close, and they need to end this before we end this?"

"*Is this* Umbrella Man?"

"My gut says no, but he's clearly a part of this." I make my decision. "I have to call Houston."

I dial him, and he answers on the first ring. "Tell me you have something to save my ass right now."

"There was a man I met on the scene, name is Mitch McAllen. Forties, salt and pepper beard. Pale green eyes. He was wearing a CSI jacket, and he was taking pictures."

"Holy fuck. Mitch was there? In a CSI jacket? That little prick."

My eyes rocket to Kane's. "Who is he?"

"A reporter. I'll handle him. I hate that piece-of-shit. If I ever committed murder, he'd be my victim, and I'd have no regrets. Anything else before I go personally beat his fucking ass? Don't say DNA testing. I'm doing it. I said I'm doing it."

"Then that would be all."

"And his name isn't Mitch McAllen. It's David Moore, but the eyes and the beard give him away. Lying sack of shit. I'll get back to you." He hangs up.

Reporter, I say, texting Tic Tac the news, adding, *Back to the drawing board.*

I'm about to type more, but stop with a thought that has me calling Houston back.

"I don't know who I want to avoid more," he answers. "You or the mayor."

"I want that reporter's DNA."

He barks out laugher. "He's no killer. He's obviously too dumb to be this killer in particular, but you know what? I'm going to enjoy asking for it. Serves him right for sneaking onto our crime scene. Done." He hangs up. I set my phone down and pick it up again to text Tic Tac: *Look for that reporter on the security feed from the other crime scenes, too.*

Kane's phone buzzes with a text that he gives a quick glance. "Kit's on his way. I'm going to give him your list." He exits the room, and I start writing out notecards again.

This time, I focus on extracting important pieces of the data Tic Tac provided, but end up doing what I have yet to do. Writing names on notecards to include: Lily, Sally, Thomas, Houston, Melanie, Roger, me, Kane, Detective Williams, each of the victims, my father, and even Pocher. I pin the victims in a row on one of my cork boards and write out details about their lives. I write out additional cards for people who donated to my father's campaign who have a direct link to this case such as Roger, Houston, and Melanie.

Also Melanie's brother, Brandon Carmichael, who is a real standout as far as I'm concerned. He might not have supplied the drug that killed the victims, but he must know how to use it. He's on Kit's list, to begin surveillance, but I text myself all of his details. I can't interview him without setting off a major red flag, but I need to see him in person. I know people. Okay, I know killers. As much as Kane wants to make me believe I'm not one of them, they see me as one of them. Ghost sure as hell does. If I get close enough to Brandon, I'll know if he's him, the man behind Umbrella Man. And there is one person behind Umbrella Man, even if he has help. This is all done in such a calculated perfect way, his way. Anyone else is support staff. This is a cause to him, a major New York stage show that he's orchestrated.

My cellphone rings with Houston's number again. "Did he confess?" I answer.

"Funny," he says. "Your always so 'not' funny. The mayor has me holding a press conference tomorrow morning. Do you want to be there? To let the public know the FBI is involved?"

"What part of stop holding press conferences do you not understand?"

"The victims include one of our own and a television star," he says. "That is high profile. On this, I get where he's coming from. It's getting press. We want to control the narrative."

"There were three victims, not two."

"Two sisters. Right. That rattles people as well."

"This is what he wants. He wants attention. He wants to be in the press."

"And he's got it. His way, not ours."

"This is my call."

"You can't stop the mayor from talking about losing one of our own or a crime spree in the city. Do you want to be there?"

"The killer wants me there." I tap my pencil on the desk and consider my options, "but you know what? Yes. I have a plan."

"Are you going to tell me that plan?"

"No."

"Is that all?"

"Yes." I hang up.

The only plan I have is to buy time, but I'm not sure I can.

It feels like this is it.

It feels like Kane and I are next.

And he's going to meet Ghost.

I stand up and head down the stairs, following male voices to the kitchen. Rounding the corner, I find Kane at the endcap and Kit and another man on the side facing my entry. I glance at the stranger, and Kane says, "Meet Zar, Lilah."

I give his short hair and thirtysomething features a once over. "I thought with a name like that you'd have long hair and wear lots of jewelry." I stop at the island across from Kit and next to Kane, focused on Kane. "I need to talk to you."

"I need to show you something first," Kit says, sliding a photo in front of me. "Kane told me who I was looking for, and I'd already flagged this guy. He wasn't with the rest of the crew that came in."

I glance down to find the same green-eyed reporter, dressed in a service uniform, inside the stairwell of this building. I grab it. "When was this?"

"During the power outage," Kit says. "We let a team in to try and repair the circuits. He had a fake ID and logged in as Miller Farris."

"I need to call Houston," I say, "and my phone is upstairs." I start to turn, and Kane slides his phone to the counter.

"You want me to call the police chief from your phone?"

"I'm highly amused by the idea," he assures me, a quirk to his lips.

"I'm sure you are," I say, but I make the call.

"Kane Mendez," Houston answers.

"No, he's just my lover," I say.

Zar laughs, which you know always earns points with me. I like people who get my jokes, especially hearing half the conversation. They're few and far between. "I have footage from our building, and your reporter asshole was here. He was dressed in a maintenance-style outfit and signed in with a fake ID."

"He's known for being sneaky," he says. "He's not the guy."

"I want him brought in for questioning," I say. "Call me when you have him, and I'll meet you at the precinct. And Houston? I've never met a killer who someone didn't think was a nice person. Don't be an idiot who gets someone killed. Assume he's the killer." I hang up.

"How many killers have you known?" Zar asks.

"More than you."

"I doubt that," he says dryly, and he actually sounds proud of that statement.

I lean on the counter and look him in the eyes, killer's eyes. "I know you. I knew you the minute you walked in the door and the only reason you're staying in my house is that I know you're riding along with Kane tonight. And I know Ghost. I've met him. He'll shoot you first." With that, I look at Kane. "I need to speak to you."

"Anything you wish, my love," he says, giving me another amused look.

I exit the kitchen, and he follows me to the bottom of the steps where I turn to face him. "I have a bad feeling about this meeting with Ghost." I press my hand to his chest. "Just hear me out. The murders were by our building and in our building. That's the perfect time to make us the next victims. And now, we even know the building isn't secure."

"This apartment is," he assures me. "Ghost called again. That's what he does. He moves things around to protect himself. I have to go now. I'm leaving Kit with you because you seem less likely to shoot him."

"Zar isn't enough backup. Let me go. I'll be your backup."

"I'm not taking you, Lilah."

"Because you think we'll both end up dead."

He cups my head and kisses my forehead before looking down at me. "Pocher is the one who is going to die. And painfully. The kind of pain I've wanted him to feel since he had you attacked. I'll be back tonight. I promise." With that, he releases me and walks away.

And I let him because I have to let him.

CHAPTER THIRTY-FIVE

Kane makes me human alright.

I'm pacing Purgatory, imagining him dead, imagining me killing Ghost in a fit of rage. Imagining the moment that I'm no longer human. Why didn't I just kill Ghost? Why the fuck didn't I kill him when I had the chance?

Loaded with adrenaline, and get to work, I call Tic Tac, and have him get me "stuff." He pulls Miller's file. I manage to occupy my mind by reading up on him. He's forty-four. He's single. He's had a domestic abuse charge. He could be the guy, at least on paper, but he doesn't feel like the guy. One of the cult, I decide. I call Houston, and he doesn't answer. My phone buzzes with a text: *Miller was an entertainment reporter for a year. He interviewed the soap star.*

I immediately dial Houston again. Twice. He answers the second time. "He's not at home or work," he says. "They can't find Miller."

"Did you go into his apartment?" I ask.

"We can't just go into his apartment," he says.

"You sure as fuck can. He was at two murder scenes and one of them he identified himself as law enforcement. And he's got a history with one of the victims. He interviewed Karen. Go in now." I eye the address of his apartment, which is across town. "Call me when they're in. I'm on my way. And tell them to glove and boot up. I don't want evidence trampled on."

"You really think this is the guy?"

"Just do it, Houston. It's raining again. He might be gone because he's at a victim's home and the way we save him or her is at his apartment." I hang up and grab my field bag. This might not be "the" guy, but he's really damn close. I just hope like hell Kane really has Ghost on a leash because I'm about to put a hell of a lot of pressure on Umbrella Man and the Society.

I hurry down the stairs to find Kit watching TV in the living room. "Let's go." I don't wait on him; I head for the door.

Five minutes later, I've updated Kit, and I'm in the back of an SUV, driven by one of Kane's men with Kit next to me when Houston calls. "He's dead, Lilah. A bullet just like the others."

"Fuck," I say. "Then he's the secondary victim. The family member who was doing things to try to keep the real victim alive. We need to know who that victim was, though, from what I read, there isn't a long list. A girlfriend. Look for a girlfriend."

"I was just told that he was Detective Williams' press contact. Maybe this really is him. Maybe he killed himself."

I digest that with a discomfort level equal to heartburn. He didn't kill himself, and this isn't over, but someone wants me to think that. They don't want me to know that I'm a future victim. They don't know Kane knows about Ghost. Someone knew that I'd found him and that information traveled through law enforcement. "I'll be at the crime scene in fifteen minutes." I hang up, grab my field bag, my damn rain jacket, and rush for the door to have a little chat with yet another dead body.

***

Thirty minutes later, I've left my raincoat at the door, pulled on gloves and I'm inside Miller's apartment that is as sterile as a hospital room. Miller is dead on his couch, blood all over the cushions, nothing clean about it. No clean freak shoots himself.

It's too messy. I walk the apartment, which doesn't take long. Like so many city apartments, it's a pair of moving boxes with the kitchen in one of them and the bathroom in the other. If there's a clue left for me, I can't find it. I go through his desk in the corner, but there isn't so much as a light bill.

I stand in front of the body and dial Tic Tac, studying the body as I listen to the rings. He was a nice-looking guy, probably got women. There has to be a girlfriend. Of course, he might have beat her out of his life.

"Lilah," Tic Tac answers. "Let me guess—"

"I need stuff. Yes. How long has Miller, who's dead by the way, lived at his residence?"

"Three years," he replies, "and holy wow, Batman."

I grimace. "I don't communicate with people who speak in such language."

"Agent Love."

I glance up to find Houston striding into the room. I hang up on Tic Tac, "Chief," I greet since we're being all formal and shit.

"Anything I need to know?" he asks.

"I need to know if he was a neat freak."

"We'll do the necessary interviews," he says. "But the mayor is ready to hold a press conference tonight. He's already put out the notice to the press."

"And say what?"

"It's him," he says. "It's over. You did your job, and you did a kickass job. Nobody had him on our radar but you."

"And the minute I did, he's dead, Houston."

"Coincidence."

"There's no such thing as—"

"Coincidence," a familiar male voice says from the doorway.

I look up to find Roger standing in the doorway. "I agree, Agent Love." He glances around. "It's too clean, quite literally. Neat freaks don't shoot themselves. It's too bloody. He would have taken the poison."

"Look, Roger," Houston says, "I respect the hell out of you but don't come in here and try to turn my crime scene into another jungle. He's dead. It's over." He looks at me. "Are you in or out on the press conference?"

"I hate lies, Chief, but if you want me there—"

"Don't be a bitch, Lilah," he snaps. "People are terrified. Scared shitless. We have extra patrols out, and the call volume is up one hundred percent for safety checks. We need to calm people down. We need to give them peace. And the fucker is dead. I'll handle the press conference." He turns and walks away.

"Alone on a deserted island," Roger says. "No one is going to believe us until another body shows up. They'll apologize soon."

I glance over at him, and I realize then that I'm not like him at all. Sure, I hate stupid people. I hate stupid actions. I like dead bodies more than the living, most of the time, but he's an example of why. The living are so damn self-serving, and I'm done always serving him. That's why I struggled with my cases with him. I was serving him, not the victim. "I don't want them to apologize, Roger. That means someone else dies. I *want* to be wrong. Something you've never been good at." I walk out of the apartment and toss my gloves and boots in the trashcan the CSI team has set up. And I don't look back. Roger belongs in my rearview mirror, and the glass is so damn broken I can't even see him anymore.

"This isn't over, Lilah," Roger says from that rearview, but I don't turn back.

He's right. This isn't over, but I'm going to end it. And I do that best without him.

CHAPTER THIRTY-SIX

The minute I'm back in the SUV, I dial Kane. He doesn't answer. Fuck. Fuck "Fuck!"

"Holy fuck," Kit says next to me. "What the hell is going on?"

"Why isn't he answering?"

"He said he'd be offline for a few hours."

"That's unacceptable." I text him: *Call me. Now.*

He doesn't call.

I text him again: *Miller, the reporter—he's dead. They made it look like he was the guy, and he killed himself to end it. It's not him, but you know they want us to let down our guard. Keep yours up.*

I text Tic Tac: *Is Brandon Carmichael on duty at the hospital right now?*

His reply is: *Checking,* and then sixty seconds later: *Yes. He's in surgery. Fifth floor.*

Send me a photo, I reply, and he does.

"Take me to the hospital," I say to the driver, sinking back into my seat. It's time to get an in-person look at Melanie's brother.

I sink back into my seat and shut my eyes, letting the rain thrum on the window, going to my Otherworld, here and now. It feels like a lifetime has passed since this started, but it's only been days. Only days since Junior left me a note. I've forgotten Junior could be a part of this. That means this started on Long Island, but that doesn't feel right.

Detective Williams is in the center of this. She didn't expect to die. She was the insider at the force or at least one of them. Where there's one gnat, there's an infestation. Someone knew I knew about Miller. Houston knew, but he told his people to take action. Houston seems to be trying to do a hellish job. He needs to grow some balls that fit a man his size, but overall, I don't think he's dirty. But, then again, I thought my father was Mr. Rogers, and he turned out to be

183

Michael Myers, and he even has the mask and the knife he shoved in my hand.

The SUV pulls up to the hospital, and I start to get out. Kit grabs my arm. "What are we doing?"

"I don't know about you, but I'm potentially having your hand for dinner."

He jerks his hand back. "I'm just trying to protect you."

"That went well for Jay. Are you trying to get a roommate situation? Because you do have good timing?"

"Lilah, please."

"Please," I say. "Please works. Hands do not. I'm visiting Jay to see if he's well enough for me to throttle him while observing a suspect. You're welcome to come, but if you screw up my surveillance, I can't be responsible for my actions."

He laughs. "I'll stay with Jay and protect him."

"Whatever toots your horn, but don't show me the horn. I never ever want to see that shit."

He laughs again. I might like him, too, but that could be short-lived. I liked Zar for about five whole minutes, though Kit is showing longevity.

I pull up the hood of my rain jacket, and Kit does the same. We exit the SUV and dart to the front of the hospital, swiping the rain from our bodies as we enter.

A few minutes later, we're at Jay's doorway watching him flirt with a pretty redhead. "He's a loser," I say. "I'd walk away."

Jay glances up. "Ding dong the bitch has arrived. But she saved my damn life. You stubborn bitch." Kit steps into the doorway and Jay adds, "You're next, man. Look out. She's trouble."

The nurse approaches, and Kit and I enter the room. I glance over at her. "He'll die for you unless you save his life."

Jay curses in Spanish, and the nurse leaves in a bout of laughter, while I join Jay by his bed, giving him a once over. "You look pale like you're not even Mexican."

"So do you," he says.

"Good one," I say. "I might have said it myself. Oh, and by the way, there's a doctor here who might be a killer who uses poison stocked in the hospital lab. It's not really poison, but misused, it works dandy."

"What the fuck? Are you serious?"

"As a nun scolding you about your sexual preferences. I'm leaving Kit here with you to talk about how to protect yourself."

"That's it," he says. "They're discharging me tomorrow. I'm out of here now." He sits up.

"Bullshit," Kit says. "They weren't letting you out tomorrow."

"I'm leaving tonight," Jay snaps.

"Good idea," I agree, and it is, which is why I came here. Well, one of the reasons.

"Meet you both in the SUV," I say, exiting the room.

I take the stairs for a reason, aside from the gabbers. It's expected that I might visit Jay. Visiting Brandon is another story. I take the stairs down three levels and exit to a waiting room. I sit down and study the photo and then wait. An hour later, Brandon walks in, and the couple in the corner hops out of their seats. I proceed to watch him cry with the couple as he shares bad news. Holy fuck, I need a drink.

That man is not the man. I don't think he could even be a part of this. I am so far from knowing what I'm doing right now that I'm like that two-year-old kid who's been all over the Internet lately with blow-up floaties on his arms. He tries to shove food in his mouth and he can't reach his mouth, but he still keeps trying. He doesn't see that he needs a new approach. I need to take off the floaties. I need a new approach. I quietly disappear into the stairwell and text Kit: *Headed to the SUV.*

A few minutes later, I'm in the backseat with Jay, and Kit is upfront. "Take Jay to our place," I say, "and then drop me at the precinct."

And that's what happens. We pull up to our apartment, and Kit takes the wheel. The driver, I don't know his name, comes around to help Jay out. "We have Rice Krispies," I say before he exits into the rain. "The snap, crackle, pop will make you feel better."

"Catch this asshole," he says. "Then I'll feel better. And yeah, well, I'll eat some Rice Krispies, too."

He gets out, and I'm shut inside the back of the SUV on my way to the station to reexamine the evidence, to find what I've missed, but I can't help but try Kane again. I punch his auto-dial. His phone goes to voicemail. Kit eyes me in the mirror, a question in his look.

I shake my head.

CHAPTER THIRTY-SEVEN

It's nine when I arrive at the station, hours after Kane left me at the apartment, and he's still silent. I'm about to lose my flipping mind, and I cannot deal with people right now. I might be arrested, which is exactly why I go straight down the stairs to the evidence room in the basement. Once there, I discover that the security desk for that room is presently unmanned, and I can't get in. I walk down the hallway to a row of offices and flash my badge at an old man behind a desk. "Where's the person running the desk?"

He takes a bite of a donut and says, "Lunch," with his mouth full as if displaying why they keep him in the basement.

"When does that person get back?"

"Just left," he says with another mouthful of donut. "Any time now. She had some dinner something or another to go to."

Just left and any time now. Brilliant. "I'll wait," I say, and I snatch a donut.

"Hey!" he growls all fierce and stuff like he might throw a donut at me or something. Which works. More for me.

I snatch a napkin, too—because a girl needs a place to set her donut and wipe her mouth—and then I head back toward the security desk. Once I'm at the old steel dinosaur, grab a pad of paper, and I write two names side by side: Pocher and Detective Williams. I draw a circle around their names and connect them. They're connected. I take a bite of the donut that is a sugary orgasm. Thank God I don't work here anymore. I'd eat them all. How does anyone expect us to sit around late at night and not eat them? Nothing else is open or fresh. How are we going to shoot bad guys without donuts? I take another bite, and I add another name and another circle. My father. I connect all three. Finally, I write Umbrella Man and repeat.

Detective Williams wasn't Umbrella Man, but she's at the core of his attacks, perhaps to help him control the setup of the victims?

My mind starts throwing out ideas, playing mental basketball to see what lands where:

Umbrella Man is an assassin.

He's Ghost.

No.

He's not Ghost.

I try to call Kane again and get his voicemail. I try Zar as well. I also get his voicemail.

"Umbrella Man is not Ghost," I murmur, which I don't know why this comforts me. The Society hired Ghost to kill Kane.

I transition that thought to a broader one: they also hired Umbrella Man.

My brow furrows.

What if the Society, through Williams, was stupid enough to think they could really turn a serial killer into an assassin? In which case, they have no real control. Any they think they have is a façade. He's smart. He'll eventually turn on them. A killer who enjoys the game. I've said that. Kane has said that. All of this tonight, the entire Miller scene, was just him playing a game with law enforcement and me, testing me to be worthy enough to continue playing.

I finish my donut while staring at all of the names I've written down. They're all the Society. Detective Williams must have had some level of authority. Maybe she even found Umbrella Man through her work. Tic Tac sent me her cases. I'm just going to have to go through them one by one. I circle her name again and write: *Redman and Morris*. Her ex who is dead, and her other ex who is a cop.

I pull up an email from Tic Tac and check the list of people who donated to my father's campaign and are connected to this case. Redman is not on the list. That would suggest he was not Society. Maybe he was just a victim Williams was setting up. What if she and Morris plotted against Redman together? Maybe they never broke up. Williams just lured Redman in and made him love her.

Really that doesn't make sense. Maybe Morris was just jealous and that made Williams the center of attention, the center of the spiral of death.

I'm officially a nutcase because either way, that would make Sergeant Morris, the little bitch baby, Umbrella Man. I have a hard time going there, but Morris *was* pissed at the crime scene last night, and the only three people in that alleyway who know he didn't kill Williams is me, Ghost, and him or her. What if he wasn't upset about Williams dying but rather having his kills challenged by another killer?

Could he really be a cold, calculated killer who hides behind his job? Could Williams, while dating him or otherwise, have found out and recruited him for the Society? I keep assuming she's the Society but maybe he really did force her into all of this. When considering his skills, the man *is* working with Roger. Roger must see skills in him that I have not, but he doesn't see Umbrella Man. Roger has clearly stated that he thinks the killer is a woman.

Something stirs in my mind, and I'm back in the lab with Roger:

My eyes meet Roger's, and he says, "You still think this has nothing to do with me?" he challenges.

I step to him. "Are you telling me you're the killer, Roger?"

"Do you think I'm the killer, Lilah?" he challenges.

"I think you're an asshole, Roger. You know that was a threat. You know what he was telling me."

"Tell me. What was he telling you?"

"Eventually, he's going to kill the people close to me and then kill me."

"That's right," he agrees. "That's exactly what he's telling you."

He repeatedly called Umbrella Man, him, not her. In the past, when he believed we were dealing with a woman, he said "her." Is he covering for him? Or maybe he doesn't want to see him as who he really is? He damn sure doesn't see me clearly. Or, maybe he's trying to catch him on his own to take credit. But at the expense of lives? The more I think about his connection to Roger, the more Morris is feeling like a suspect.

I stand up. I need to get home and go through his case files and look through Morris' cases as well. I need to look for people he killed and covered up. But I also need in that evidence room. If I can just look at what was there last night again, maybe something will click. I walk back down the hallway, and now, everyone is gone.

I take the stairs several floors to the main desk that operates in the evenings and shove my badge under the gate between me and the officer there. "I need in the evidence room."

He glances at my badge and then says, "Oh, right. Agent Love. I have a package for you. The guy who came in said you'd want this tonight. I was about to try and reach you."

He shoves an envelope under the gate. "But I don't have the evidence room key. You have to check-in in the basement."

It's me. I'm the little bitch right now; because as I hold that package, some part of me instinctively knows it's from Umbrella Man, and I'm all but shaking. Kane hasn't answered my calls, and I'm terrified, yes, terrified, that I'm about to find out why.

CHAPTER THIRTY-EIGHT

I walk to the bathroom and shut the door. I don't bother to lock it; I won't be in here that long. I open the envelope and toss the contents in the sink. A badge wallet falls out. I glove my hands and pick it up, flipping it open, and I am instantly brittle with cold. Detective Williams' ID is inside, but there's also a plastic badge with a slice of paper across the center that reads: East Hampton. Where my brother is chief of police. Andrew. Mother of God, my brother is next. We didn't talk after I warned him to be careful. I didn't check on him. Why the hell didn't I check on him? With a quake to my hand, I shove the badge in the bag again and then dial my brother.

Ring.

Ring.

Ring.

Voicemail.

"Call me now, Andrew. It's urgent." I text him the same message.

I grab the envelope, exit the bathroom and walk to the guard behind the gate again. I shove it under the bottom. "Bag it and send it for fingerprints and do it now. Call me if there's a match. And I mean now." I'm all about now right now, and I don't wait for confirmation. I turn and start walking.

I hurry outside and thank fuck, it's not raining. By the time I'm down the steps. Kit's pulled the SUV to the curb. I climb in the backseat, and Lord help me, I still have on the gloves.

"Take me to the airstrip," I order, bagging my gloves. I don't give him an address. The one Kane uses works just fine for me. "And break the fucking speed limit."

He turns around. "I don't think that's a good idea. We need to wait for Kane."

I pull my gun and point it at him. "He has my brother, so if you think I won't shoot you and shove you out of the way to drive, think again."

He curses and turns around, doing what he should have done in the first place, drives. I dial Kane. He doesn't fucking answer. "Kane, you need to call me. Please. I'm saying please. Fuck Ghost. Tell him I said so. They're going after Andrew. Umbrella Man is going after Andrew. I'm getting a chopper to the Hamptons and taking Kit with me." I hang up and dial Andrew again. He doesn't answer.

I dial my father. "Lilah?" he answers. "What the hell? It's late and—"

"Where is Andrew?"

"I don't know," he snaps. "He's a man, not a boy and—"

"Listen to me, and listen carefully. Your 'friends' hired a killer. He's a *serial* killer, not a damn assassin. You don't control serial killers. He's supposed to come after me, and I wouldn't be surprised if you knew."

"Lilah—"

"I said listen, and you better fucking listen. This is a game to him, and he's playing it his way. He's going after Andrew. He might already be dead. Call Pocher, and you tell him to pull the serial killer back and do it now. If he even can. And don't go hunting for Andrew. Stay where you are and pull your security tighter."

He's silent three beats. "I don't know what this is, but I'll call. I'll find out what I can." He hangs up.

He doesn't know my ass. I dial Kane again. I dial Andrew again. No one is fucking answering. I could call the precinct and send someone to look for Andrew, but I feel like I would be sending someone to their death. Maybe I'm even triggering the moment Andrew dies. "Kit, I need one of Kane's men in the Hamptons to—"

My phone rings, and it's Kane. Oh God, it's really Kane. I kind of want to cry right now. "Kane," I answer. "Thank God."

"I'm on my way to you. I'll meet you at the airstrip. I'm about twenty minutes out. I already called and got a chopper."

"I can't wait. You know I can't wait."

"He wants you there, Lilah. This is a trap. You can't go without me. You *will not* go without me."

"I *cannot* wait for you. A few minutes could be the end of him. If he's not already gone. And I'm only three minutes out. Don't you have a man watching him?"

"Yes, I do."

"That's it? Oh fuck. You can't reach him."

"Wait on me, Lilah. Please, beautiful. Wait."

I can feel myself dying inside. Andrew. Not Andrew. "I can't wait. But I love you, Kane. In all your dirty, dark, wonderful ways, I fucking love you." I hang up.

"He's going to kill me if I don't stop you," Kit says.

"I'm going to kill you if you try," I say, declining Kane's returned call. "So you can decide, Kit. Die now or die later."

He curses and pulls us into the airstrip parking lot that, at this time of night, is a ghost town. I'm out of the door before he even puts it in park, holstering my weapon as I slam the door shut. I walk inside the building and into an empty waiting area. Kit joins me, and we walk to the desk. "I need the chopper you have reserved for Kane Mendez," I tell the woman behind the counter.

The woman, a brunette with her hair pulled back so tight it looks like she could bust an eyeball, puffs up. "I'm sorry, but we have strict instructions—"

Kit groans. "Jesus, Lilah."

I slap my badge on the counter. "FBI business. I need that chopper now."

CHAPTER THIRTY-NINE

It's raining again.

I sit in the chopper and watch it pound the windows. Kit is next to me, clinging to his seat and looking like he might keel over. And all I can think is that this godforsaken weather needs to just go away. How many days can a sideswipe of a late-season hurricane create this kind of downpour? Too fucking many considering Umbrella Man seems to like this shit.

I spend the duration of the flight thinking through everything that might happen on the ground. I don't let myself think about Andrew being dead. When we finally land and I'm in the lobby of the airport, I have a voicemail from Kane: *By the time you hear this, I'll be in the air coming for you. Wait for me, woman, but since I know you aren't going to fucking listen, there's a car waiting on you with one of my men. Fernando's a good man. The man guarding your brother was one of my best, too, but he's still off-grid, which is why I sent Fernando to you. Safety in numbers. And I didn't want to risk Fernando being the reason Umbrella Man did something he hasn't already done. Andrew's alive. You stay alive. I love you, Lilah. Damn it, stay alive. Kill him.*

I disconnect and tell Kit, "Fernando is waiting for us." At just that moment, a tall Hispanic man walks into the room.

"Fernando," Kit confirms, and I'm fast to cross to his position. "Anything from your man here on the ground?"

He gives a grim shake of his head. "Nothing."

"Because he's dead," I say.

His expression is grim. "He's my brother."

Kane had one brother guard the other. And now, he knew the two siblings fighting for their siblings would fight well together. Kane knew that would win me over, and he's right. It does. "Then let's go get our brothers back."

He nods and the three of us exit to the driveaway, where a black SUV idles, light rain falling. "Go to the chief of police's office," I say before I run to the front of the vehicle and climb inside. Fernando follows to take the wheel while Kit settles in the back.

I dial Andrew.

No answer.

I try his desk at the chief's office.

No answer.

I call my father back.

No fucking answer. If he warned Umbrella Man I'm coming, I might kill him myself.

Fernando doesn't ask me for an address, but five minutes later, we're at the station where four cars are parked and the lights are on, too many cars for this time of night. One of the cars is my brother's. "That's Andrew's car."

"That means my brother is here," Fernando says, glancing at me. "Because we never desert those we protect. That's Kane's rule. Kane is good to me," he adds. "You don't die today." He pulls up his hood and starts to get out.

I catch his arm. "Don't be a hero. Follow my lead."

"We're not going in the front door."

"We're at the front door. He knows we're here. The best way to take him off guard is that I go through the front."

"I'm going through the front with you," Kit says. "The end."

"I've got the rear," Fernando says, and I nod my approval. If Kit is with me, Umbrella Man may not expect Fernando.

I yank my hood into place and exit into the rain, my hand settling under my rain jacket to rest on my weapon. Kit is by my side at the front of the vehicle, and we wait for Fernando to make it around the building before we start walking toward the door.

Once we're there, out of the line of view of the windows, Kit pulls his weapon. I reach for the door, and he comes over my shoulder to aim. Kane's men are better than half the law enforcement I've worked with. I open the door and listen.

There are four cars outside and not one voice. Not one sound of movement.

I pull my weapon and force myself to mentally settle into my zone. I am not Andrew's sister right now. I'm an FBI agent. I enter the building, which forces me into a narrow hallway. I ease forward, stepping lightly, and glance in the office around the corner. Ralph Norton is face down on his desk. Fuck. Fuck. Fuck. Fuck. I fight the urge to call out to Andrew. I fight the urge to run forward and just find him now. I hold up a hand at Kit and then glance back and motion to the office, pointing my finger at my head to tell him what's going on.

His jaw sets, and he nods. I move forward again and motion for him to check the man down. He slips away behind me. I bring a galley of offices into view. There are three dead officers, one leaning back in a chair with a bullet in his forehead. Another face forward on a desk. One on the floor. None, I realize, are Andrew, and I feel no guilt for my relief.

Fernando enters and comes toward me down a hallway. "Anything?"

I motion toward my brother's office, and Kit rejoins us. "They're all dead." He eyes the office and us. "I'll go." Weapon in hand, he moves forward and steps into the room. I can't even breathe as I watch him enter. Fernando pants out a breath feeling the same.

Seconds tick by before Kit steps out of the office, a grim look on his face. "Your brother isn't here, Lilah." I have a moment of relief before he looks at Fernando. "Yours is."

Fernando balls a fist on his forehead and murmurs in Spanish before charging forward. He starts forward. I don't stop him. It's a crime scene. It needs to be secured, but I just don't have it in me to deny him this moment of grief. And this ends tonight anyway. I follow Kit, and I enter the office to find Fernando leaning over his brother on the floor. My gaze lifts and lands on the desk. There's another badge wallet there. Holy hell. I cross to the desk, grabbing a pair of gloves and a bag before I flip it open. It's Andrew's badge. It's an invitation to go to Andrew's house.

CHAPTER FORTY

I dial the neighboring station. "Sheriff Jack here, how can I help you?"

I know Jack. He's a good guy. "Jack, it's Lilah Love. FBI Agent Lilah Love."

"Well hell, Lilah L—"

"Listen to me. I pursued a killer here. I'm at my brother's office. He's gone, and his people are dead."

"Oh shit. Shit. Shit. Shit."

"Deep breath and listen. I don't have time to chase down the rest of his officers. I need you to come here, secure this crime scene and get them all here safely. The perp is a serial killer. Do not, I repeat, do not try to help me catch him. I need to handle this. One mistake and people die. Do you understand?"

"Andrew?"

My chest burns. "I don't know. He was kidnapped to get to me. Come now and do not blow this." I hang up and motion to Kit and hold up the badge. "It's an invitation I'm accepting. You coming?"

"Hell yeah, I'm coming."

Fernando stands up, his shirt stained in blood. "I'm coming."

"You're too emotional."

His jaw clenches. "I don't get too emotional. Ever. I do, however, get even."

The look in his eyes is familiar. It's me. I get it. Kane understood it when he connected us. This man's brother died trying to save my brother. He deserves his revenge. "Then let's go," I say, leading the way down the hallway and we step into the lobby.

I push open the door, and a downpour greets me. I have a flash of me on the beach in the rain, stabbing my attacker. Déjà vu. I have a sense of coming full circle. The three of us pile back into the SUV, and Fernando drives us to my brother's house, or rather, a little cottage a few miles from my place just off the beach. He used his inheritance to buy it, and he loves that damn cottage. Fernando parks a block down and kills the engine and lights. "He knows we're coming. We're walking into a trap."

"Yep," I say, pulling up my hood and getting out of the vehicle, drawing my weapon as I do. Rain pummels me, but I push through it. Kit and Fernando frame me.

"I'm going straight in the front door," I say. "He won't expect me to come at him directly. That means you two come at him when he's off center. The property is gated. We'll go over the gates. Both of you go over the top." Neither argue with me.

We reach the gate, and they each split away from me and disappear in different directions. I climb over and land in mud, but I could give two shits. He knows I'm coming, but I want those few seconds he would expect to have with the security gate beeping. Once I'm there, I pull my weapon and peak in the window. There is no movement. That is until I see Fernando enter through an open patio door.

"Damn it," I murmur, reaching for the door. It's not locked. I enter, and suddenly it's me, Fernando, and Kit standing in near silence, but for a tick of my mother's favorite grandfather clock. I motion one left and one right again, and a knot forms in my belly. No sound. No confrontation. He might already be dead.

I head up the stairs toward the only room there— Andrew's bedroom, holding my breath as I enter. He's not here, but there is something on the bed. I ignore it, for now, walking to the closet and the bathroom to find them both clear.

I return to the bed to find a picture of my mother lying there. My cottage used to be my mother's. I grab it and run down the stairs, shouting, "They're at my place!" already headed to the front door. The bastard is playing with me, telling me all the law enforcement in the world and Kane's men can't stop him. Telling me he has all the time in the world, but my brother does not.

CHAPTER FORTY-ONE

I hold the picture of my mother in my hand, and I wonder if this asshole killed her, if that's part of his message. Fernando parks a block from my cottage as he had at my brother's. I fold the photo and stick it in my pocket before I reach for the door. Fernando catches my arm. "What's the plan?" he asks.

I don't bite off his hand. He's had enough pain today. "I'm not making an arrest today. We kill the fucker. We *kill* him."

"All right," he says and releases me, reaching for his door while Kit curses. My cellphone vibrates in my jacket pocket, but I let it ring. It's Kane. He'll tell me to wait. I'm not fucking waiting. I exit to what is now a light drizzle, and I start walking with my new army at my side. Once we're at my property, I don't even think about sneaking up to the door. I wouldn't be here if I didn't get his message.

With both men by my side, I walk right up to the front door, but when we get there, Kit cuts around the side of the house. Fernando and I share a look, and I open the door. It waves open, and I can see straight through to the open patio door. He's on the beach with my brother. The same damn beach where I was raped, where I killed my attacker. He's telling me he knows it all. He's telling me he planned it all. My mother's murder, which is why we're at my mother's house. My attack at my mother's getaway home. Rage burns inside me, but it's a comfortable rage that fits like a glove. It's not wild. It's not erratic. It simply sits in the deepest part of my chest and waits to be unleashed.

I start walking while Fernando cuts left to search the rest of the house because he doesn't get it. They aren't in here. They're on the beach. I cross the living room and exit the house to the patio. Rain drizzles around me, but I leave my hood down. I step outside the overhang, and in a few steps, I can see my brother there on the beach, on his knees, a gun in his hand. He's alive and that's the gift that keeps on giving. A man stands behind him, holding a gun to his head.

I want to run to Andrew. I want to save him. But I walk slow, steady, calculated until I can finally make out the man: it's Sergeant Morris.

There is no satisfaction in me about being right about his identity. There is just my readiness to kill him. "Stay back, Lilah!" Andrew calls out. "Stay back!"

I don't stay back. I keep moving, aware of the lights on the water near the dock half a mile away, certain that is how he got to the island, certain that is how he plans to leave, though I'm not sure how he thinks he'll ever make it the boat. Just that he has a plan. He thinks he's leaving. He's not. "That's close enough!" he shouts when I'm two feet away from the spot where I killed that bastard who raped me. Where I'm going to kill him as well.

I halt and say, "Throw your weapon down."

The rainfall quickens, and I am momentarily back in that night, that man on top of me, his sticky, sweet breath sickening, the drugs drowning me. I tried to fight. I couldn't move. This time. I can move. This time, I'm not drugged.

"Throw down your weapon!" he shouts.

I don't throw my weapon down, but I do lower it to my side. "What is this, Morris? What are you doing?"

"Ending this. That's what they want. An ending. You're as much trouble as your mother was."

"He killed her," Andrew says. "He killed mom. And he killed all those people to make it look like we're victims of a serial killer."

He killed mom.

The confirmation is brutal. She was murdered. "He *is* a serial killer," I say. "Pocher hired him to kill for them."

"And granted me an army," he gloats. "Because you just wouldn't stay out of his business. Because you just couldn't appreciate his plan to make your father President one day. I told him I could end you and Kane, and your brother here as a bonus. And here we are. Because I'm sick and fucking tired of hearing Roger talk about how good you are. This is how good you are. I was right under your nose, and you didn't know it. And now, you're about to watch your brother die before you die."

Kane is dead.

No.

Kane is not dead.

But Pocher must think he is. Ghost must have told Pocher he killed him. And Pocher told Morris.

My mind races with plans A, B, and C but discards them all.

Morris laughs, a cackling sound. "They tried to kill you right here on this beach, now, didn't they? And all that fool they hired got was a fuck out of you before you killed him. He wasn't me."

"Lilah?" Andrew says. "What is he talking about?"

I ignore Andrew, I buy time, I keep going back to plan A and telling myself it's a mistake. "What did Detective Williams have to do with this?"

"Pocher's side bitch. She'd do anything for him and his money. Fuck me. Kill her sorority sister."

"Why Redman? Why'd you pick him?"

"Lilah!"

It's Kane, and Morris's gaze lifts wide and then goes to his hand where he's holding something. That's all the opportunity I need. Plan A it is. I lift my gun and shoot him between the eyes. Yes. I'm that good a shot. Being raped created an obsession with killing after all. I needed the skills to do it. At the same time I fire, an explosion rips from behind me. Everything is in slow motion. Morris falls to the ground. Andrew and I both fall to the ground. My head rattles but I push to my feet, to find Andrew doing the same. I turn, and I'm dragged into Kane's arms only to watch my mother's house burning to the ground, and I know in my gut, that this was the distraction Morris planned to get to his boat, to escape. My eyes go wide. The boat. Someone was on the boat. I shove out of Kane's arms and turn to find the boat speeding away.

Whoever was on it is gone.

"Call the Coast Guard!" I shout as law enforcement overwhelms the scene. "The boat!"

Andrew grabs me, hugs me and whispers, "I love you,"
in evident good physical condition before he says, "I'm going
to make sure Pocher gets picked up before he can run." He
takes off running, and I turn to find Kane on the phone,
stepping to him as he asks, "Is it done?" I don't miss the
disposable phone. "Excellent. Until next time." He
disconnects and pockets the phone. "Pocher is dead.
Another victim of Sergeant Morris."

I digest that with bittersweet victory. He ordered my
rape. He ordered my murder, twice, and that of my brother.
"He killed my mother. Or he ordered her death. Morris said
he did."

"And now he'll burn in hell."

I nod and turn to stare down at Morris, fighting unease.
Kane's hands settle on my shoulders from behind. "It's over,
Lilah."

And yet, it doesn't feel over at all. After all this time, it
was too easy. I feel like there's more, but then, there always
is more. If there is anything my rape taught me, it's that I
never stop living it. I will never be over it. This will never be
over.

CHAPTER FORTY-TWO

It's hours later, dawn is breaking on the horizon, and I'm staring at my house, my mother's house, now a shell of what it once was, while firefighters work to clean up. Kane is with me, his arm around my shoulders. "We'll rebuild it."

"No," I say, turning to him. "This was where she ran from my father. This is where she hid from his nastiness. This is where I was raped. I don't think that's a part of her life she needs remembered. How is Fernando?"

His lips thin. "He gave a statement and then headed to the city to tell his mother. I don't envy him."

A car pulls up, and halts. The doors open and Director Murphy, along with Chief Houston, step out. They head our direction and Kane murmurs, "Do you want me to leave?"

"Fuck them," I say. "You stay. They can leave."

He gives a low chuckle, and the two men step in front of us. "Agent Love," Murphy greets. "Good to see you in one piece." His gaze shifts to Kane. "And Kane Mendez," Murphy says, offering up his hand. "Good to have you by our beast of an agent's side."

Kane shakes his hand with ease. "As I always will be," he assures him.

Houston's expression sours. "The coast guard caught up with the boat. It was a Spanish speaking hired hand. We don't believe he was involved beyond a paycheck." He doesn't give me time to reply. "You okay, Lilah?"

"I'm fucking amazing," I say. "He's dead." But even as I say the words, it doesn't feel right. He doesn't feel like Umbrella Man, and I just can't shake that feeling.

"So is Pocher," Murphy informs me.

My gaze rockets to his. "Is he?"

I swear Murphy smiles without actually smiling. "He is. Apparently, Morris killed him."

"He and Williams were having an affair," Houston tells me. "Once we got into Morris's apartment—which was insanely OCD by the way—we found a shrine to Pocher and Williams on his walls." His lips thin. "There were a lot of people on his walls. They were in color-coded segments that appear to be the way he murdered them. He changed it up, so he wouldn't seem like the same person. He's going to be studied for years to come."

Director Murphy motions me aside, and the amusement in his eyes is hard to miss. He's leaving Kane with Houston, and he loves it. I follow him a few feet to a tree. "When one falls, another will rise, but it will take time. We, *you*, slowed them down."

"He told me that Pocher killed my mother. Or he ordered the murder."

"And he turned on Pocher?" he asks, but the glint in his eyes says that he knows better. He knows what we did.

"Seems that way," I say.

"Indeed. Well just know this Agent Love, Pocher was near the top of the chain, but he was not *the* top of the chain. Nor was he one of a few. They are many. Don't forget that." His hand comes down on my shoulder. "But you, you are making the difference that I knew you would make. I'm just sorry it came at the cost of so many good officers tonight."

"As am I."

"I'll stick around a few days. I'll go back to the city for meetings. This is your rodeo." He turns and walks away, while another car pulls up to meet him. Yet another arrives, this one a police vehicle, and my brother gets out.

I walk to meet him at his door, noting Kane and Houston are actually in what appears to be a deep conversation. That's as likely as a damn cow laying an egg, and yet, it's indeed happening. "How are you?" I ask as I join Andrew.

He scrubs his jaw. "I lost some good men tonight. It's going to be a rough week.

I need to do a press conference. How about we do it together tomorrow?"

"Together," I agree. "Let's do more of that."

"Yes. Let's." He hugs me and pulls back. "You talk to dad?"

"No. You?"

"I talked to him. He knows about Pocher. I assume you know about Pocher?"

"I do. He was evil, Andrew. I tried to tell you that."

"I should have listened."

"Then listen now. The people he worked for still exist. They may or may not continue to support dad, but together, we need to pull him back."

"They're going to support him, Lilah. He already got a call about protecting his campaign. That's what he wanted to talk to me about when I was dealing with the loss of lives. When you and I almost lost our lives."

And there it is. Proof that it's not over.

As Murphy said, when one falls, another rises.

Houston joins us, and we game plan on the press conference and the press that will follow that. We just killed a serial killer. *I* just killed a serial killer. Houston is about to leave when he says, "Truce. I called a damn truce with Kane. For you, Lilah. For you, because of what you went through tonight and in the past." He turns and walks away.

My gaze shoots to Andrew's. "Did you tell him—"

"No. I can't tell anything I don't know. Because you never talked to me about a rape, Lilah."

"And I never will."

He nods in understanding. "I hope my personal life doesn't affect that."

"I hate your girlfriend. I love you. And now that you might actually listen when I talk, I might talk. One day."

"She moved to LA. She's gone, Lilah."

"Oh. How very disappointing."

He laughs. I laugh. And the laughter is enough for now. I turn and walk toward Kane who is waiting on me. "Houston called a truce?"

"So he says."

"My father already has new Society support."

"Of course, he does," Kane says.

"One falls—"

"And another rises, but we'll win, Lilah. Because we have you and your badge to keep us in the middle, where we belong."

CHAPTER FORTY-THREE

After six weeks of chaos, I'm on a boat not far from the Hamptons home I now share with Kane when we're not in the city. I sit on the top level, bundled up in jeans and a sweater, watching the storm clouds that are holding us back from launching, the first storm in weeks. It's a chilly day that isn't too brutal, and Thanksgiving is only a week from now, but there is nothing like brisk ocean air and champagne with Kane Mendez. And below deck, it's nice and toasty. Not to mention, Kane and I both need this getaway.

There has been press. There have been funerals. There has been far too much interest in me and Kane, considering Kane's lifestyle, as well as me as my father's daughter. The father I don't speak to. Just once since Pocher's death. And that was far from cordial. There's Roger, who wants to be in the press over this far more than I do, so I let him. At one point, Kane and I sat and watched him on a hot nighttime news channel talk about serial killers and Morris who he knew was no match for me, and I had to turn it off. Every time I start thinking about Morris, something nags at me.

"You're thinking about him again," Kane says. "I thought the idea of unplugging on the ocean was not thinking about him."

"You're right," I say, "And don't get used to hearing that. I just can't shake the idea that it was a cult operation run by one person who wasn't Morris."

"The DNA at the crime scenes matched his."

"That doesn't make my theory invalid."

"It is, however, off limits this weekend, remember?"

"Yes. I remember." This weekend is our time. No press. No drama. Just us.

He downs his champagne. "Let me give you something else to think about. I have two gifts for you." He reaches in his pocket and pulls out a square velvet box. "That's number one."

I down my champagne and accept it.

"Before you open it," he adds. "That's to represent our past, to hold onto every moment we've ever had. The second gift is about our future."

"Now I'm curious." I reach over and touch his cheek. Human. God, how this man makes me human. I open the lid and stare down at a gorgeous diamond necklace. I glance at him. "It's stunning and ridiculously expensive. How is this our past?"

"It's your first engagement ring. I had it turned into a necklace."

"My first? Well, my only because—"

He goes down on his knee in front of me. "Because you have a new one, for a new life with me, filled with honesty at all costs." He presents me with another box. "Marry me, Lilah. This time really fucking do it." He pops the lid to display a gorgeous pink and white diamond in an oval setting "Pink?" I laugh.

"To remind you that you don't have to be tough with me. To remind you that I see all those parts of you that you hide from everyone else, and I love them."

I actually tear up. "God. You're going to make me cry, and you know I don't fucking cry."

"Answer?"

"Yes. Yes, of course, I'll marry you. I'll really fucking do it this time."

"Yes, you will," he says and places the ring on my finger. Next, he settles the necklace around my neck. "I want to go downstairs and look at it in the mirror," I say. "And pee."

He smiles and kisses me while thunder rumbles above our heads. I now have a new reason to love thunder, rather than so many reasons to hate it. I hurry downstairs, and I've actually got a gift for Kane, too. It's a coin that I saved from our first trip overseas together. I wanted it to be a message, a way to tell him that I never let go. I admire my necklace and ring and then walk to my bag in the bedroom, and manage to grab my badge. I stare down at it and pull out the photo of me and Kane I keep behind it. I turn it over and stare at the marks I've made there; one for everyone I've killed. Morris has his own mark. Morris the Umbrella Man.

Or not.

"Damn it," I murmur and shove the photo back into place. This weekend is not about that shit.

I grab the coin, which is also in a velvet box. I then hurry above deck to find it raining, but Kane hasn't come inside for shelter. I stick the box in the front pocket of my sweater and round the deck.

That's when I go cold. Kane is on his knees, and Roger is holding a gun to his head. There's a knife in each of his front shoulders, deep enough that if yanked, it might kill him. The world fades in and out. The past flies through my head, to all the games Roger made me play. To his mix-up of pronouns—him and her—when talking about Umbrella Man. I'm suddenly back in the same memory I've visited several times in the past, back to that day at Melanie's office that had bothered me:

"Do you think I'm the killer, Lilah?" he challenges.

"I think you're an asshole, Roger. You know that was a threat. You know what he was telling me."

"Tell me. What was he telling you?"

"Eventually, he's going to kill the people close to me and then kill me."

"That's right," he agrees. "That's exactly what he's telling you."

The reason I didn't worry about Roger being hunted by Umbrella Man is that, on some level, I knew it was him, but as Kane said—I have always let Roger fuck with my head. "Lilah, leave now," Kane whispers. *"Leave now."*

I stay focused on Roger. This is between me and him—mentor and protégé. "You know that he has security everywhere, right, Roger?" I challenge.

"Not today," he says. "Today, you two were headed off to the ocean and safe as could be." He motions to his white pants and white shirt. "I dressed for the occasion, all crisp and clean. And I'm not the one getting dirty today."

"What do you want?"

"For you to finally become who I've been grooming you to become. For you to finally accept the killer that you are, that I always knew you were."

"I'm not a killer like you."

"Just a killer like you?" he challenges. "I tested you. That night you were raped, I said if she's like me, she'll kill him. And I watched. And you did."

"You set it up."

"Of course I set it up. Morris was a pansy. He didn't kill any of those people. I did. He wanted money, lots of money, and Pocher gave it to him. He wanted to disappear. You handled that for me." He taps a knife at his waist. "I called your brother. He's on his way. I told him I'm going to kill you. I told him he could save you but to come alone. He will. We both know he will." He grabs the knife and offers it to me. "Kill Kane, accept who you are, and I'll spare your brother. You can kill me and take over the throne. But you have to kill Kane. You have to show me you really don't feel love."

He knocks one of the blades in Kane's shoulder. Kane grunts, but I don't react. Roger is sick. He's really fucking sick, and there is only one way to win his games. The same way I won in the alleyway months ago. I play. I win. "Lilah," Kane says, "do what you need to do and don't feel any guilt."

I don't look at him. Roger tosses the knife between me and him. "Pick it up." He then steps behind Kane. I walk to the knife and pick it up. I need to feel like a killer because I'm about to be one, and I remember the moment I drove that blade into my attacker. I imagine it. I enjoyed it. My gaze goes to Roger's. "I'm ready. Are you?"

"I've been ready. I've been waiting for you."

I walk forward, slowly, cautiously, certain Kane knows what to do. I stop in front of Kane, and I grab one of the knives in Kane's shoulder. "Should I take this out?" I ask Roger.

He laughs. "Do it how you want to do it."

I look down, the fatal mistake Morris had made, but it's all part of the game. Kane grabs Roger's legs, and I reach over Kane and slam the knife into Roger's chest. He gasps and drops the gun, and I end up on top of him. I don't even know how that happens, but it doesn't matter. Morris killed no one. Roger did. He killed my mother. He attacked Kane. I start stabbing him and stabbing him. Over and over and over, until Kane pulls me off of him. "Lilah. Lilah, he's dead."

I pant out a breath and another and then drop the knife. My white sweater is covered in blood. He's dead. Roger is dead and he needed to be dead. I wait to feel remorse. I wait to feel guilt. I feel none of those things. I turn and grab Kane's waist, the knives still jammed into his flesh. "My phone. We need an ambulance. You need help."

Kane catches my leg with his, holding me to him, keeping his hands free. "As long as the knives stay in, I'm safe. I can move my arms. He didn't go deep and he didn't hit nerves. I got lucky and leaned forward when the bastard snuck up behind me and jammed the knives in my shoulders."

"You think. We don't know."

"I'll call a doctor I know. He'll come to us. Right now—"

"We need to get rid of the body."

"I'll do it, Lilah. Unless you want to call the police this time, but think hard. Think hard because—"

"We'll do it," I say. "I'm not losing my badge over Roger. Together, right?"

"You're sure?"

"Yes. I'm sure. I'm so fucking sure."

"Holy hell," Andrew curses.

I turn to face him and he's now on the deck, pointing a gun at Kane. "What is this?" he demands. "Lilah. Lilah, are you okay?"

"I stabbed him," I say. "He's Umbrella Man. He killed mom, and Kane was—is—put the fucking gun down, Andrew!"

"She stabbed him twenty times," Kane says. "Do you know what this means? Do you know what that will do to your sister's life?"

Andrew looks at the body and then at me. "He's the one?"

"He's the one," I say. "He did it all."

His lips thin and he looks skyward, before he holsters his weapon. "Then we need to get rid of the body."

And so, I watch my brother and my future husband decide how to get rid of Roger's body.

And they do.

And we do.

And that is my version of Happily Ever After, at least for now. This will fuck with my head. If I believe Roger, I might be a female Dexter. The Society will keep coming at us. The cartel will keep coming at us. Junior will likely write me another note. Meanwhile, I think I'll wear pink to my wedding. Serial killers don't wear pink. Because I'm fucking doing it this time. I'm marrying Kane Mendez.

THE END

***

WHAT'S NEXT FOR ME? TANGLED UP IN CHRISTMAS, A SEXY STANDALONE COWBOY ROMANCE RELEASES NEXT WEEK ON THE OCTOBER 29TH! AND FOLLOWING THAT, THE FINALE TO MY NAKED TRILOGY, TWO TOGETHER, RELEASES IN NOVEMBER, AND MY BRAND-NEW SAVAGE TRILOGY LAUNCHES IN DECEMBER WITH SAVAGE HUNGER!

TANGLED UP IN CHRISTMAS (OCT. 29, 2019)

TWO TOGETHER (NOV. 19, 2019)

SAVAGE HUNGER (DEC. 17, 2019)

***

KEEP READING FOR THE FIRST CHAPTER OF A PERFECT LIE, MY FIRST PSYCHOLOGICAL THRILLER, AND THE FIRST CHAPTER OF ONE MAN— THE FIRST BOOK IN MY NEW NAKED TRILOGY!

***

DON'T FORGET, IF YOU WANT TO BE THE FIRST TO KNOW ABOUT UPCOMING BOOKS, GIVEAWAYS, SALES AND ANY OTHER EXCITING NEWS I HAVE TO SHARE PLEASE BE SURE YOU'RE SIGNED UP FOR MY NEWSLETTER! AS AN ADDED BONUS EVERYONE RECEIVES A FREE EBOOK WHEN THEY SIGN-UP!

HTTP://LISARENEEJONES.COM/NEWSLETTER-SIGN-UP/

A PERFECT LIE

I am Hailey Anne Monroe. I'm twenty-eight years old. An artist, who found her muse on the canvas because I wasn't allowed to have friends or even keep a journal. And yes, if you haven't guessed by now, I'm that Hailey Anne Monroe, daughter to Thomas Frank Monroe, the man who was a half-percentage point from becoming President of the United States. If you were able to ask him, he'd probably tell you that I was the half point. But you can't ask him, and he can't tell you. He's dead. They're all dead and now I can speak.

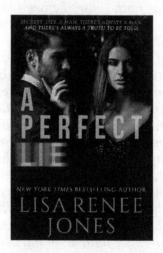

CHAPTER ONE OF A PERFECT LIE

Hailey Anne Monroe

You already know that I'm one of those perfect lies we've discussed, a façade of choices that were never my own. But that one perfect lie is too simplistic to describe who, and what, I am. I am perhaps a dozen perfect lies, the creation of at least one of those lies beginning the day I was born. That's when the clock started ticking. That's when decisions started being made for me. That's when every step that could be taken was to ensure I was "perfect." My mother, a brilliant doctor, ensured I was one hundred percent healthy, in all ways a test, pin prick, and inspection could ensure. I was, of course, vaccinated on a strict schedule, because in my household we must be so squeaky clean that we cannot possibly give anything to anyone.

Meanwhile, my father, the consummate politician, began planning my college years while my diapers were still being changed. I would be an attorney. I would go to an Ivy League college. I would be a part of the elite. Therefore, I was with tutors before I could spell. I was in dance at five years old. Of course, there was also piano, and French, Spanish, and Chinese language classes. The one joy I found was in an art class, which my mother suggested when I was twelve. It became my obsession, my one salvation, my one escape. Outside of her. She was not like my father. She was my friend, not my dictator. She was the bridge between us. The one we both adored. She listened to me. She listened to him. She tried to find compromise between us. She gave me choices, within the limits I was allowed. She tried to make me happy. She did make me as happy as anyone who was a puppet to a political machine could be, but the bigger the machine, the more developed, the harder that became. And still she fought for me.

I loved my mother with all of my heart and soul.

That's why it's hard to tell this part of my story. If there was one moment, beyond my birth, that established my destiny, and my influence on the destiny of those around me, it would be one evening during my senior year in high school, the night I killed my mother.

***

THE PAST—TWELVE YEARS AGO...

The steps leading to the Michaels' home seem to stretch eternally, but then so do most on this particular strip of houses in McLean, Virginia, where the rich, and sometimes famous, reside. Music radiates from the walls of the massive white mansion that is our destination, the stretch of land owned by the family wide enough that the nearest neighbor sees nothing and hears nothing. They most certainly don't know that while the Michaels are out of town, their son, Jesse, is throwing a party.

"I can't believe we're at Jesse's house," Danielle says, linking her arm through mine, something she's been doing for the past six years, since we met in private school at age eleven. Only then I was the tall one, and now I'm five-foot-four to her five-foot-eight, and that's when I'm wearing heels and she's not.

"Considering his father bloodies my father on his news program nightly, I can't either," I say. "I shouldn't be here, Danielle."

She stops walking and turns to me, her beautiful chestnut hair, which goes with her beautiful, perfect face and body, blowing right smack into my average face. She shoves said beautiful hair behind her ears, and glowers at me. "Hailey—"

"Don't start," I say, folding my arms in front of my chest, which is at least respectable, considering my dirty blonde hair and blue eyes are what I call average and others call cute. Like I'm not smart enough to know that means average. "I'm here. You already got me here."

"Jesse doesn't care about your father's run for President," she argues. "Or that his father doesn't support your father."

"Why did you just say that?" I demand.

"Say what?"

"Now you've just reminded me that I'm at the house of a man who doesn't support my father, whom I happen to love. I need to leave." I start down the stairs.

Danielle hops in front of me. "Wait. Please. I think I might be in love with Jesse. You can't just leave."

"My God, woman, you're a drama queen. You have never even kissed him. And I have to study for the SAT and so do you."

"Please. His father isn't here. His father will never know about the party or us."

"Danielle, if my father finds out—"

"He's out of town, too. How is he going to find out?"

"What about your father? He's an advisor to my father. You can't date Jesse."

She draws in a deep breath, her expression tightening before she gushes out, "*Hailey,*" making my name a plea. "I'm trying so hard to be normal. I know that you deal with things by studying. I do, but I need this. I need to feel normal."

Normal.

That word punches me with a fist of emotions I reject every time I hear it and feel them. "We will never be normal again and you know it. We weren't normal to start with. Not when—"

"After that night," she says. "We were normal enough until then. But since—after what happened, after we—"

"Stop," I hiss. "We don't talk about it. We don't talk about it *ever.*"

"Ouch," she says, grabbing my hand that is on her arm, my grip anything but gentle. "You're hurting me."

I have to count to three and force myself to breathe again before my fingers ease from her arm. "We agreed that 'the incident' was buried."

"Right," she says, and now she's hugging herself. "Because we're so good at burying things."

"We have to be," I bite out, trying to soften my tone and failing. "I *know* you know that."

She gives me several choppy nods. "Yes." Her voice is tiny. "I know." She turns pragmatic, her tone lifting. "I just need more to clutter up my mind than the SAT exam. That will come and go."

"And then there will be more work ahead."

"I need more," she insists. "I need to be normal."

"You will never—"

"I can pretend, okay? I need to *feel* normal even if I'm not. And even if you don't admit it, so do you."

My fingers curl, my nails cutting into my palms, perhaps because she's right. Some part of me cared when I put on my best black jeans and a V-neck black sweater that shows my assets. Some part of me wanted to look as good as she does in her pink lacy off-the-shoulder blouse and faded jeans. Some part of me forgot that the "normal" ship sailed for me the day I was born to a father who aspired to be President, but still, I don't disagree with her. I need to get her head on straight and maybe kissing Jesse is exactly the distraction that she needs do the trick. I link my arm with hers once more. "Let's go see Jesse."

She gives me one of her big smiles and I know that I've made the right decision, because when she's smiling like that no one sees anything but beauty which is exactly how it needs to stay. And so, I make that walk with her up those steps, climbing toward what I hope is not a bad decision, when I swore I was done with those. Nevertheless, in a matter of two minutes, we're on the giant concrete porch, a Selena Gomez song radiating from the walls and rattling my teeth.

The door flies open, and several kids I've seen around, but don't know, stagger outside while Danielle pulls me into the gaudy glamour of the Michaels' home, which is as far opposite of my conservative father as the talk show host's politics. The floors are white and gray marble. The furniture is boxy and flat, with red and orange accents, with the added flair of newly added bottles, bags, cups, and people. There are lots of people everywhere, including on top of the grand piano. It's like my high school class, inclusive of the football team and cheerleaders, has been dropped inside a bad Vegas hotel room. Or so I've heard and seen in movies. I've not actually been to Vegas; that would be far too scandalous for a future first daughter, or so says my father.

"Where now?" I ask, leaning into Danielle.

"He said the backyard," she replies, scanning. "This way!" she adds, and suddenly she's dragging me through several groups of about a half-dozen bodies.

Our destination is apparently the outdoor patio, where a fire is burning in a stone pit, and despite it being April, and in the sixties, surrounded by a cluster of ottoman-like seating and lanterns on steel poles. Plus, more people are here, and now instead of Selena Gomez rattling my teeth, it's Rihanna.

"Danielle!" The shout comes from Jesse, who is sitting in a cluster of people to our far left. Of course, Danielle starts dragging me forward again, which has me feeling like her cute dog that doesn't want to be walked. Correction: Her forgotten dog that doesn't want to be walked, considering she lets go of me and runs to Jesse, giving him a big hug. I'm left with one open seat, smack between two football players: David Nelson and Ramon Miller. Both are hot. Both have dark hair, though Ramon's is curly and excessive, and David's is buzzed, understandably since I think I heard his dad is military. Okay, I know his dad is military because I've been crushing on him since he showed up at school six months ago.

I sit awkwardly between them, and stare desperately at Danielle, who just stuck her tongue down Jesse's throat in a familiar way that says it's not the first time. *I need to leave*, I think. I'll just get up and leave, but then, what if she panics? What if she forgets that Jesse can't be in on 'the incident'? We can never tell anyone what happened. Why did I think this night was a good distraction?

"Hey there," David says, piercing me with his blue eyes.

"Hi," I say.

"You look like you want to crawl under a rock," he comments.

"Do you know where I can find one?"

He laughs. He has a good laugh. A genuine laugh and since I don't know many people who do anything genuinely, I feel that hard spot in my belly begin to soften. "I'll help you find one if you take me with you."

"You don't belong under a rock," I say.

He arches a brow. "And you do?"

"Belong," I say. "No. But happier there right now, yes."

"That hurts my feelings," he says, holding his hand to his chest as if wounded.

"Oh. No. Sorry. I just meant...I don't do parties."

"Because your dad is a politician," he assumes.

"He doesn't exactly approve of events like this."

He laughs again. "Events. Right." His hand settles on my leg and there is this funny sensation in my belly. "I'll make sure nothing goes wrong. Okay?"

"No. No, I'll make sure nothing goes wrong."

He leans in and presses his cheek to mine, his lips by my ear. "Then I'll give you extra protection." I inhale, and he pulls back, suddenly no longer touching me.

My gaze lifts and I find Danielle looking at me with a big grin on her face. David hands me a shot glass and Jesse hands Danielle one. She nods, and I don't know why, but I just do it. I down the liquid in what is my first drink ever. The next thing I know, David's tongue is down my throat and when I blink, I'm not even sitting on the back patio anymore. I'm lying on a bed and he's pulling his shirt off. And I don't know how I got here. I don't know what is happening. Panic rises with a sense of being out of control. I stand up and David reaches for me, but I shove at him.

"No!"

I dart around him and I must be drunk but I think my feet are too steady to be drunk. I run from the room and keep running down a hallway and to the stairs. I grab the railing, flashes of images in my mind. David offering me another drink. Me refusing. David kissing me and offering me yet another drink. I had refused. So why was I just on a bed and unaware of how I got there?

"Hailey!"

At the sound of David's voice, I take off down the steps, not even sure where I'm going, but I don't stop. I push through bodies and I'm on the porch in what feels like slow motion. I'm running down the stairs. I'm leaving. I have to get out of here.

***

I blink awake, cold, with a hard surface at my back. Gasping with the shock of disorientation, I sit up, the first orange and red of a new day in the darkness of the sky. I'm outside. I'm...I look around and realize that I'm on the bench of a picnic table. I'm in a park. I stand up and start to pace. I'm dressed in black jeans and a black sweater. The party. I went to the party. I dig my heels in. Did I get drunk? Wouldn't I feel sick? I'm not sick. I'm not unsteady. My tiny purse I carry with me often is at my hip. I unzip it and pull out my phone. Ten calls from my mother. No messages from Danielle.

"Danielle," I whisper. "Where is Danielle?"

I dial her number and she doesn't answer. I dial again. And again. I press my hand to my face and look at the time. Five in the morning. My car is at Jesse's house. I start walking, looking for a sign, anything to tell me where I'm at. Finally, I find a sign: *Rock Creek Park*. The party was in McLean. Rock Creek is back in Washington, a good forty minutes away. I lean against the sign and my mother calls again.

I answer. "Mom?"

"Thank God," she breathes out, her voice filled with both panic and anger, two things that my mother, a gentle soul, and doctor, who loves people, rarely allows to surface. "Oh, thank God. I've been so worried."

"I don't know what happened, Mom. I blacked out and I'm at a park."

"Near Rock Creek," she says. "I know. I did the 'find my phone' search but it's not exact and I was about to call the police. I just knew—" She sobs before adding, "I just knew you were dead in the woods. I was about to get help. I was about to have a search start."

"I—Mom, I—"

"Go to the main parking lot." She hangs up.

My cellphone rings with Danielle's number. "Where are you?" I demand.

"At Jesse's," she says. "Where are you? I was asleep and I thought you were in a room with David, but he was with some other girl."

224

"You don't know what happened to me?" I ask.

"No. Jesus. What happened?"

Headlights shine in my direction from a parking lot. "I'll call you later," I say. "I have to deal with my mother." I hang up and start running toward the lights. By the time I'm at the driver's side of my mother's Mercedes, she's there, too, out of the car and reaching for me.

"You have so much to explain," she attacks, grabbing my arms and hugging me. "I am furious with you. You scared me."

"I scared me, too," I say hugging her, starting to cry, the scent of her jasmine perfume, consuming my senses, and calming me. "I don't know what happened."

She pulls back. "Did you drink and do drugs?"

"No. I mean—one drink. I'm fine. I—"

"One drink. We both know what that means. This wasn't the first time."

"No. Mom. It was. One drink. I don't know what happened. Someone drugged me. They had to have drugged me."

Her lips purse. "Get in the car."

"Mom—"

"Get in the car."

I nod and do as I'm told. I get in the car. The minute she's in with me, I try to explain. "Mom, I—"

"Do not speak to me until I calm down." He seatbelt warning beeps.

"Mom—"

"Shut up, Hailey," she says, putting us in motion.

I suck in air at the harsh words that do not fit my mother, who is not just beautiful, but graceful in her actions and words. Perfect, actually, and everything I aspire to be. I click my belt while her warning continues to go off. She turns us onto the highway and I listen to the warning going off, trying to fill the blank space in my head with answers I can give her. But there are none and suddenly she lets out a choked sound and hits the brakes. My eyes jolt open, but everything is spinning. We're spinning. I can't see or move. "Mom!" I

225

shout, I think. Or maybe I don't. Glass shatters. I feel it on my face, cutting me, digging into my skin.

We jolt again, no longer spinning, but the world goes black.

Time is still.

And then there are sirens and I try to catch my breath, but my chest hurts so badly. "Mom," I whisper, turning to look at her but she's not there. She's not there. Panic rises fast and hard and I unhook my belt and ball my fist at my aching chest. Forcing myself to move, I sit up to find my mother on the hood of the car, a huge chunk of steel through her body.

I scream and I can't stop screaming. I can't stop screaming.

ORDER A PERFECT LIE HERE:
HTTPS://APERFECTLIEBOOK.WEEBLY.COM

THE NAKED TRILOGY

BOOK ONE IS AVAILABLE EVERYWHERE NOW! BOOKS TWO AND THREE ARE AVAILABLE FOR PRE-ORDER!

One man can change everything. That man can touch you and you tremble all over. That man can wake you up and allow you to breathe when life leaves you unable to catch your breath. For me that ONE MAN is Jax North. He's handsome, brutally so, and wealthy, money and power easily at his fingertips. He's dark, and yet, he can make me smile with a single look or word. He's a force when he walks into a room.

Our first encounter is intense, overwhelmingly intense. I go with it. I go with him and how can I not? He's that ONE MAN for me and what a ride it is. But there are things about me that he doesn't know, he can't know, so I say goodbye. Only you don't say goodbye to a man like Jax if he doesn't want you to. I've challenged him without trying. He wants me. I don't want to want him, and yet, I crave him. He tears me down, my resistance, my walls. But those walls protect me. They seal my secrets inside. And I forget that being alone is safe. I forget that there are reasons I can't be with

Jax North. I forget that once he knows, everything will change.

Because I need him. Because he's my ONE MAN.

CHAPTER ONE OF ONE MAN

Jax...

The moon glows with white light and hangs low and round over the nearby ocean darkened by night as if it, like the hundreds of guests in the garden of one of the San Francisco Knight hotels, is watching the beautiful brunette and star of the night. Emma Knight, the twenty-eight-year-old heiress to the hotel chain's worldwide empire, and who, in fact, lost her father one month ago. Now, her brother Chance rules their hotel empire and her mother has fled to Europe for reasons few, I suspect Emma included, knows.

But I know.

She stands next to Randall Montgomery, her brother's right-hand and confidant, a man who might be fit enough and decent enough looking if he didn't act like he has a stick up his ass. A man on my radar for reasons he'll soon regret. He wants Emma and her money. She is the furthest down the food chain of them all, and based on her history with her father, even further down than would be expected. No doubt, she inherited with her father's death, but I wouldn't be shocked to discover she was given a token instead of a goldmine.

The announcer stands at a podium and begins lavishly speaking of Emma's father with purpose. Tonight, with women in fancy gowns and men in tuxedos, ice carved into sculptures and champagne poured in glasses, Emma is here to accept a philanthropy award on his behalf while her brother is curiously absent. If he were here, I wouldn't be here. Neither I nor any of the North family could stand her father, not that I find her brother any more palatable. Her father is gone, though, and now Emma is the proverbial queen of the hour. And the queen, unaware that she is, has had my attention for quite some time.

There's irony in the fact that I, Jax North, the eldest now of the living North family offspring is, in fact, the man who watches her. An irony she'll understand soon, but not too soon. For now, I stand at one of the rows of white-clothed tables, deep enough beyond in the crowd of people to be as good as in the shadows, a man whose family has done business with her family for decades, though l have been in the shadows in those endeavors just as I am here now. Present but unseen.

Emma steps to the podium, but not before I catch a glimpse of her pale pink floor-length dress that is elegant in its simplicity, in the way it highlights her slender but womanly figure. Her hands grip the sides of the podium and for a long moment, a full minute at least, she simply looks out across the crowd but doesn't speak. There's a charge of expectation in the room, a sense of the crowd pushing her to speak and when finally, her pink-painted lips part, the microphone crackles and squeaks. This seems to jolt her and she laughs nervously, a soft sweet laugh to match her sweet little ass. Perhaps the only sweet things about the Knight family.

"Thank you all for being here," she finally says, and her voice is strained but suitably strong. "It's emotional to be here tonight, among those honored who are living while my father is no longer with us. To be here at a hotel that was the center of the world for him." She cuts her stare and I can almost feel her struggling for composure, the way I struggle when I speak of my older brother.

"I loved my father so very much," Emma adds, and the pain in her voice is it for me. I run a hand over the silk of my light blue tie, barely contained impatience in the action, but tonight isn't the time; it's not when I'm meant to find Emma and Emma me. It's a thought that has me turning away and disappearing into the gardens, entering the hotel by a side door. I'm here in this hotel for one reason: Emma. She's here and it's long past due that we meet. It's long past due that she learns about the connection between her family and mine. I stroll a carpeted hallway with elegant chandeliers dipping low at strategic locations, about to turn into the bar when I come face to face with Eric Mitchell, a man who is quite literally a genius. He's also vice president in one of the largest corporations in the world.

"Long time, man," he greets, offering me his hand. It's a strong hand, and when I look into his blue eyes, I see the man born a savant, the man who see numbers more than words. I see the man who helped Bennett Enterprises reach beyond a legal powerhouse to a conglomerate, even before acquiring an NFL team.

"Doesn't Bennett own hotels, which would make you the Knights' competition?"

His lips curve. "Keep your friends close and your enemies closer. I went to school with Chance. Good guy."

Good guy my fucking ass. "We should talk."

"About?"

"All things green. How about lunch tomorrow?"

"I can make that happen. "

We set-up the meeting and the ways this little encounter has inspired me are many. I cut right into a dimly lit bar that's desolate at the moment and thank fuck for it. The damn hotel is filled to the rim for that awards ceremony. Alone suits me just fine right about now and I walk to the back of the bar and sit down in a red leather booth that overlooks a room with couches, cushy chairs, and dangling lights but also provides a curtain for privacy. The Knight name is all about luxury and comfort, but at its core, it's about greed. At my core right now, I'm about that speech Emma was giving, about the pain at its core. That pain is why I'm here.

A waiter appears and I order whiskey, North Whiskey, my family's whiskey, which is in every Knight hotel in the country and beyond. I don't give a fuck if it stays or goes or I wouldn't be here. "Bring the bottle."

He's just filled my glass, and the glass is at my lips when Emma walks into the bar. Alone. She's done her time on stage and ran for cover. The hotel might be hosting the event, but she isn't. She's halfway into the bar when voices sound behind her. She peeks over her shoulder and then with a panicked look, darts in my direction.

To my surprise—and I don't surprise easily—she slides into the booth with me and pulls the curtain shut. "So sorry," she says, claiming the seat next to me. "I really need to avoid a conversation and well, breathe a moment or ten. The only way to do that is to be having a private meeting that looks as if it's just that: private, not to be disturbed." She takes my glass and downs my whiskey.

Interesting that she didn't run to Randall for comfort, but in fact ran away from him.

She glances at me, and when her beautiful pale green eyes flecked with amber meet mine, there is a charge between us, an awareness that parts her lips and has her turning away from me. Because she knows who I am?

"I'll buy that bottle of whiskey for you," she says, "for letting me intrude."

A statement that either proves she has no idea who I am or that she's playing me the way a Knight will play.

It doesn't really matter. It's like the sky opened up and delivered her right to me. "Considering I'm a North and that's North Whiskey," I say, refilling the glass. "I think I can handle paying for the bottle and helping the lady of the night hide out."

Her eyes go wide. "You're Jax North." She blinks. "Of course you are. You look like the North family, all tall, blond, and handsomely brooding." She drinks a bit more. "And that's the whiskey making me overly verbal. My father didn't approve of me being overly verbal."

Except she just downed that whiskey and hasn't been drinking all night. She's nervous, rambling in a rather charming, vulnerable way that I find attractive, for reasons I don't try to understand.

"I didn't know 'overly verbal' was a thing."

"You didn't know my father well, then. Actually, no one did." She swallows hard. "Back to you." It's a hard push from any question I might have made about that statement "no one did." "You really do look like your father and brother. I can't believe I didn't immediately place you."

"You mean Hunter, I assume, since my younger brother, Brody, beats to his own drum. A drum that doesn't include running the core whiskey operation or any involvement with the Knight Hotel brand."

"Yes, Hunter," she says, and there's a flicker in her eyes, an understanding that we're talking about a brother that is no more with us on this earth than her father. "I met them both, briefly. I ah—"

I narrow my eyes on her waiting for her to finish that sentence, prodding when she does not. "You what?"

"You—"

"Lost them both, as you did your father," I supply. "Yes. My father to a ski accident, a year ago next week. Six months ago next month for my brother." I leave out the cause of death. That isn't a place either of us wants me to go with the Knight family tonight. "And yes," I add, "time helps, but anyone who tells you it makes the cut heal is lying. It just stops the bleeding."

"Thank you for saying that," she says in a deep breath, "because if one more person tells me time will make it better, I might scream." She softens her voice. "I'm sad to say that I barely knew your father and brother, and only know you now because of this moment in time, that you neither chose nor invited."

"Should I have?"

"Why would you? You don't know me." She laughs a bitter laugh. "Well, there is my family money. That's what everyone knows and wants. They think they know my worth, but they know nothing."

I don't ask what that means. I dare to slide closer to her. I dare to allow my leg to press to hers, the current between us charming the air. "I am a North, which means that I have power and money. I don't need yours."

"Money feeds greed. What you have is never enough."

"There are other things to want besides money."

"Do you know who I am?"

"Emma Knight."

"Can I deny that perhaps for the rest of my life?"

I lean closer, the scent of her distinctly warm—amber and vanilla, I believe—my interest in this woman piqued in both expected and unexpected ways. "Why would you want to?"

"A complicated answer to a simple question." Her voice cracks and she turns away from me. She reaches for my glass again and downs every drop in it. She sets it down.

"More?" I ask.

She glances over at me. "Yes, but I should warn you that I'm a very bad drinker."

I refill the glass and sip before handing it to her. She stares at the glass before her gaze lifts to my mouth. Unlike moments before, she's now thinking of exactly what I intended: about her mouth where my mouth was moments before. "I promise to catch you if you fall," I say softly.

"Don't start this relationship off by making promises you won't even try to keep."

Relationship. She's planning on this encounter leading to more, which of course could simply be because I'm now in charge of my family empire, not just the contact for all things both North and Knight. Or perhaps it's more. I plan to make it more.

"I never make a promise I don't keep," I say, and I will catch her if she falls, because once I catch her, she's mine. Once she's mine, everything comes full circle.

"Never?"

"Never," I assure her, "which is something my friends value and my enemies dread."

"Do you have many enemies?"

"A man or woman with money and power always has enemies."

Her cellphone rings and she pants out a breath. "Of course. They're now looking for me by calling me." She pulls her cell from her purse and glances at the number.

"Randall?" I ask.

Her gaze jerks to mine. "How do you know that and him?"

"I know a lot of people. Enemies everywhere, Emma," I say softly, and I find myself really wanting her to listen. Really wanting to protect her, which is a contradiction to everything I would do otherwise where the Knights are concerned. "And this one wants to be in your bed. If he isn't already."

"How do you know that?"

"I told you. I know a lot of people and things."

She sets her phone on the table without answering him. "You aren't going to answer?"

"No. I'm not going to answer. I'm not ready to go back."

"Would like to get out of here?"

"And go where?"

"A castle by the ocean."

She laughs. "If only."

"I'm serious, Emma. Come with me. I'll take you away."

"Would you be asking me that if I walked away from it all?"

The curtain pulls back and Randall is standing there, his dark hair slicked back, his gaze sliding between the two of us and landing on me. "What the fuck are you doing here, Jax?"

My lips quirk. "Enjoying good company and good whiskey." I glance at Emma. "With a beautiful woman," I add.

I expect her to blush and look away, but she doesn't. For several beats she just looks at me, her stare unreadable, but the crackle in the air between us, the whip and pull of attraction, is damn near palpable.

"Emma," Randall snaps, "you have people here honoring your father."

"Right. Responsibility calls." Her eyes, her sea-green eyes meet mine. "Thank you, Jax. For the company and the fine whiskey." Randall offers her his hand, but she ignores it and stands up.

"Don't you want the answer to your question?" I ask.

She glances behind her, over her shoulder, to meet my stare. "Yes, I do." But she doesn't stay for an answer. She walks away, doing the impossible, considering she's a Knight and I'm a North, as she does. She makes me crave more of her, but that changes nothing. I came here, seeking her out, for a reason. That reason hasn't changed.

LEARN MORE AND BUY HERE:
HTTPS://NAKEDTRILOGY.WEEBLY.COM/

ALSO BY LISA RENEE JONES

THE INSIDE OUT SERIES

If I Were You
Being Me
Revealing Us
His Secrets*
Rebecca's Lost Journals
The Master Undone*
My Hunger*
No In Between
My Control*
I Belong to You
All of Me*

THE SECRET LIFE OF AMY BENSEN

Escaping Reality
Infinite Possibilities
Forsaken
Unbroken*

CARELESS WHISPERS

Denial
Demand
Surrender

WHITE LIES

Provocative
Shameless

TALL, DARK & DEADLY

Hot Secrets

Dangerous Secrets
Beneath the Secrets

WALKER SECURITY

Deep Under
Pulled Under
Falling Under

LILAH LOVE

Murder Notes
Murder Girl
Love Me Dead
Love Kills

DIRTY RICH

Dirty Rich One Night Stand
Dirty Rich Cinderella Story
Dirty Rich Obsession
Dirty Rich Betrayal
Dirty Rich Cinderella Story: Ever After
Dirty Rich One Night Stand: Two Years Later
Dirty Rich Obsession: All Mine
Dirty Rich Secrets

THE FILTHY TRILOGY

The Bastard
The Princess
The Empire

THE NAKED TRILOGY

One Man
One Woman
Two Together (November 2019)

ABOUT THE AUTHOR

New York Times and USA Today bestselling author Lisa Renee Jones is the author of the highly acclaimed INSIDE OUT series.

In addition to the success of Lisa's INSIDE OUT series, she has published many successful titles. The TALL, DARK AND DEADLY series and THE SECRET LIFE OF AMY BENSEN series, both spent several months on a combination of the *New York Times* and USA Today bestselling lists. Lisa is also the author of the bestselling LILAH LOVE and WHITE LIES series.

Prior to publishing, Lisa owned multi-state staffing agency that was recognized many times by The Austin Business Journal and also praised by the Dallas Women's Magazine. In 1998 Lisa was listed as the #7 growing women owned business in Entrepreneur Magazine.

Lisa loves to hear from her readers. You can reach her on Twitter and Facebook daily.

CPSIA information can be obtained
at www.ICGtesting.com
Printed in the USA
LVHW042120270220
648406LV00005B/955

9 781091 111462